A Jura for Julia

A Jura for Julia

Ken MacLeod

Illustrations by

Fangorn

NewCon Press
England

First edition, published in the UK August 2024
by NewCon Press
41 Wheatsheaf Road, Alconbury Weston, Cambs, PE28 4LF, UK

NCP333 (hardback)
NCP334 (softback)

10 9 8 7 6 5 4 3 2 1

ISBN: 978-1-914953-82-8 (hardback)
978-1-914953-83-5 (softback)

Cover Art and all internal illustrations by Fangorn
Editing and typesetting by Ian Whates
Cover layout by Ian Whates

Contents

Nineteen Eighty-Nine

It was a hot, muggy afternoon in June, and the telescreen was sounding fifteen. Winston Smith jolted out of his doze. Even in the Chestnut Tree Café, even after lunch and a quarter of a bottle of Victory Gin, it was vital to feign alert attention to the hourly news.

He barely had time to gather his wits and gulp a mouthful of gin before a triumphant trumpet note brayed from the screen. Important news! A victory! But where? The fronts were quiet. For months now, no victories had been claimed. Defeats were never announced, but the growing number of discharged soldiers on the streets told the story.

'Midnight in Beijing,' the announcer intoned. 'We bring you, live from the Eastasian capital, shocking scenes of a people's rising mercilessly crushed by the ruthless guardians of a cruel oligarchy.'

Flames of a burning armoured personnel carrier flickered. Silhouettes of troops carrying rifles rushed across the screen. Machine-gun fire rattled. Screams echoed.

'Earlier today, a massive peaceful demonstration pleaded with the tyrants of Eastasia for a mere fraction of the rights enjoyed by the proud citizens of Oceania and those of its staunch Eurasian ally!'

The scene cut to daylight in a vast plaza, many times larger than London's Victory Square. The buildings surrounding it were proportionately imposing. Mounted on the wall of one of these ornate, antique edifices was a gigantic portrait of a visage clear-eyed and calm, stern but benign, with black hair swept back from a high forehead and broad temples. Only the Oriental cast of the features, and the absence of a moustache, distinguished it from the familiar face of Big Brother. That was the appearance. The reality could not be more different. Big Brother was the beloved leader of Oceania, whose wisdom and foresight compelled even the most recalcitrant to adore. This image was of Number One, the despot blindly worshipped by the teeming, regimented masses of Eastasia, who obeyed his every whim like human ants.

Swarms of these human ants, in their characteristic blue uniforms, filled the square. Many of them carried banners and placards scrawled with the incomprehensible ideograms of their barbarous jargon. Discordant shouts and chants, hungry faces contorted with anger. Near the front of the crowd a pale papier-mâché effigy of a crowned, robed female figure bobbed and swayed, its right arm upraised with fist clenched. Winston recognised it, with a shock, as a crude representation of the Statue of Victory in New York.

'Bet you they're about to burn or hang her,' someone said, in a tone of lascivious anticipation. 'Typical of these benighted Asiatics and their hate rallies.'

Something familiar in the voice made Winston turn around. A small, scrawny man sat at the next table, hunched over an empty ashtray and a full glass of gin. He had large protuberant eyes and a shock of white hair. His hands trembled slightly as he lit a cigarette. He seemed to have just arrived; he must have slipped in just after the bulletin had started, and had missed the context.

'No, it's –' Winston began. The man turned. His eyes widened.

'Smith!' he said, in a low but eager voice. 'I didn't expect to find *you* here!'

It was Syme from the Research Department. His face was

thinner than Winston remembered, and his teeth whiter and more prominent: a set of dentures, new ones, not yet settled in. They made him look like... Winston gave the thought a convulsive wrench. Syme looked like a half-starved squirrel. A squirrel; yes, that was it.

'But you were –' Winston glanced over his shoulder.

'Vaporised?' said Syme. 'So I'm told. In fact I was sentenced to ten years in a labour camp, on Shetland. Just been released. Seven years early!' He shook his head. 'Incredible.'

Incredible it certainly seemed, though no more so than Winston's own survival. For the past four years he had fully expected a re-arrest, a show trial, a walk down a white-tiled corridor and a bullet in the back of the head. At first he had longed for it: to die loving Big Brother. Later he had come to resent the inexplicable delay. Now he dreaded the quietus.

Unable to reply, Winston gave Syme an apologetic glance and looked back at the telescreen.

'They certainly seem angry,' he said, as if picking up the previous exchange.

Suddenly, out of the front row of the seething crowd, a hurled speck arced like a perfectly bowled cricket ball. The object struck the gigantic portrait of Number One, and splashed a vivid black stain, like a slanted exclamation mark, across the nose and one cheek.

The twenty or so patrons and waiters watching agog in the Chestnut Tree gasped. There was something shocking about such lèse-majesté, even against the hated leader of the enemy. The Beijing crowd too fell silent in front of the defaced portrait, as if shaken by the enormity of what one of them had done. After about thirty seconds, a single voice cried out:

Numeh Wan Sha Lai! Numeh Wan Sha Lai!

One by one, other voices joined in. Within a minute the chant was taken up by all. Fists pumped rhythmically, placards waved frantically, and the ersatz Statue of Victory jumped frenziedly up and down above the heads of the crowd.

'"Number One Shall Lie"?' Winston puzzled aloud.

Syme leaned across the gap between the tables. 'Aha!' he said, tapping his long nose. 'It means "Down with Number One". Curious, isn't it, that the name was taken directly from English?' The man had always fancied himself something of a linguist.

'"Down with Number One",' Winston repeated, in a whisper.

Syme jumped to his feet. His chair clattered to the floor behind him.

'Down with Number One!' he shouted.

Everyone turned and stared at him. Winston knew what they were thinking. The news bulletin, and therefore the policy of the Party, was evidently on the side of the rebellious crowd. Number One was the target of patriotic hate and fear throughout Oceania. But joining in this unprecedented display of disrespect and revolt felt like disloyalty. It had a shudder of blasphemy, of breaking a taboo – for reasons impossible to articulate, or even to formulate clearly to oneself.

There was another consideration. Syme had for several years been an unperson. Winston knew that, and he could be sure others here did too. Now that Syme had reappeared, his disappearance must have been expunged from the records. To treat him as suspect could itself be seen as disloyal. Yet, at some level, like Winston himself, Syme must still be under a cloud. At least two of the waiters present at any one time would be members of the Thought Police. It was all a complicated, delicate calculation, in which one mistake would be both easy and deadly.

'Down with Number One!' someone roared. 'Down with Number One!'

Winston looked around, and realised to his horror that he was now on his feet and the cry had come from him. A waiter glanced at him, then at another waiter, then at the telescreen.

The announcer's tone had become even more sombre: "'Down with Number One!" they chant. Then, after a few hours of tumult, the inevitable response…'

The screen cut to a phalanx of Eastasian soldiers, submachine guns held across their chests, tramping forward in implacable ranks. The viewpoint swung around as the column cut through the crowd, and then was stopped by the press of blue-clad bodies. How thin and frail the civilians seemed, how sturdy the soldiers! At a yelled order they turned to face outward, their submachine guns now at the ready. The outer files dropped to one knee and took aim, while the next inner files levelled their weapons above their comrades' heads.

Another shout: perhaps a warning. If so, it was either not heard or not heeded. The crowd continued to press in. You could see arms stretched towards the soldiers, and here and there fists raining blows on some luckless trooper.

The next order was given as a single scream. Its translation was provided by a storm of submachine gun fire. The fusillade scythed through the crowd at waist and head height. Bodies fell in swathes. Waves of panic spread outward.

One part of Winston's mind observed this with cool detachment, almost with scientific curiosity. There was a fascinating similarity to ripples from several stones dropped in a pond, interacting, interfering, rebounding and reflecting…

Another part was overcome with horror and pity and blind rage. He was pounding the table and shouting, over and over:

'DOWN WITH NUMBER ONE!
DOWN WITH NUMBER ONE!'

And this time, the whole café joined in. The shouts were rhythmic, deafening, making the gelid haze of cigarette smoke that filled the air quiver. The paroxysm was as collective and focused as the Two Minutes Hate, and passed as quickly.

The sanguinary scene on screen ended. All in the café fell silent, shaken and not looking at each other, half-frightened, half-ashamed. The telescreen was still droning on: '…complete collapse of morale in the Eastasian armed forces… strikes and mutinies reported across Eastasia… gallant Eurasian allies moving troops to Mongolian border… floods of refugees…'

Winston let the voice roll over him as he fumbled his overturned chair on to its feet, sat back down, and finished his gin. He was shaking, with – as he realised after a moment's introspection – relief that he had not found himself shouting 'Down with Big Brother!'

Syme, too, finished his gin in silence. He waved away the hand of the waiter who came by with the bottle.

'Duty calls!' he said, with forced cheer. He stood up, swaying a little, and fixed Winston with a smile. 'They've given me my old job back, you know,' he said. 'Still working on the Eleventh Edition, would you believe?' He shook his head, smiling wryly, as if attributing the unending delay in the final, definitive version of the Newspeak Dictionary to his own unfortunate absence for the past four years. Then he gathered his wits and brushed his palms. 'Well, these residual obsolete usages won't eliminate themselves!'

'Don't you mean, "Oldspeak wordforms unself update"?' Winston chuckled. In the old days, they had sometimes amused each other with such gratuitous translations.

Syme pondered, eyes wandering vaguely, then guffawed. 'Very good, Smith!' He tapped his nose. 'Watch your step, old man.'

Out Syme went, into the hot and noisy street, watching his step. Winston accepted the offer of more gin – the waiter in his white jacket was still hovering – and strove to rekindle the woozy

well-being he'd almost attained before the news bulletin.
Soothing tinny music trickled from the telescreen.

Once again, he'd almost reached the desired haze when he was
jolted out of it by the telescreen's hourly bray. Again he focused,
making an even greater effort at attention, genuinely eager to hear
more news of the momentous upheaval in the enemy's capital.

There was none. At the hour of sixteen, the vaunted triumph
was an increase in the chocolate ration to fifty grams a week.
Winston was hardly more startled that any reference to the
Beijing revolt had been dropped than by the distinct recollection
that the previous ration had been thirty grams. For once, the
claimed increase was real. Or it would be, if it was implemented.

The thought of chocolate induced a sudden pang of hunger.
Winston ordered a sandwich. To his surprise it arrived on white
bread, with crisp lettuce and tomato and a couple of slices of
warm bacon. Inner-Party quality, this!

The sandwich wouldn't be enough to soak up the afternoon's
gin, but it would sustain him on the journey home. He left the
café at sixteen-forty-five with almost a spring in his step. The
Tube rattled and groaned. It was not yet rush hour. Walls of
broken tiling and flickers of unreliable lighting trundled by,
station after station. He toiled up the hundred and fifty steps at
his stop, pausing for breath several times, then made his way
along the homeward streets like a sleepwalker. The grim bulk of
Victory Mansions had just hoved into view when Winston
became aware of the quiet engine-growl of a vehicle behind him,
matching his pace, and at the same time of booted footsteps
swiftly catching up. In the split second of terror he knew exactly
what to expect. Rough hands grabbed his elbows, his feet were
kicked from under him, and he was lifted in the air and flung
sideways like a sack of potatoes through the open rear door of
the black–

He'd expected a van. For the first time in his life, he was in a car. Not only was he not in one of the vans of the Thought Police: he was in one of the limousines of the Inner Party, and its top levels at that.

He sprawled across leather, knees in the foot-well, his head colliding with a central arm-rest. Someone kicked at the soles of his feet, not to hurt them but to shove them inside. The car door slammed. A black-gloved finger rapped a partition.

'Drive on,' said a voice from across the arm-rest. Winston knew without looking who spoke. It was O'Brien.

There was a sense of smooth acceleration, somewhat belied by the grinding and cracking noises as the car's evidently tough tyres crunched over broken glass.

'Seat yourself,' said O'Brien, impatiently. 'Don't grovel on the floor.' After a pause, he added darkly: 'There'll be time for that.'

Awkwardly, Winston complied. The side windows were of darkened glass, as was the partition. The seat was comfortable, but a chill gripped his bowels. He swallowed, on a suddenly dry mouth.

'What do you mean?' he croaked.

O'Brien shot him a sidelong, sympathetic glance. 'You have a most unpleasant ordeal in prospect, I'm afraid.'

'Why?' Winston cried, despite himself. 'I've confessed everything! What more do you want? A trial? I'll say anything! Get it over with and give me the bullet – I've been looking forward to it for years.'

'Indeed you have,' said O'Brien. 'You may be surprised to know that it was I who denied you that satisfaction.'

Winston indulged a moment's frantic fantasy of flinging himself out. He knew, without testing it, that the car door would be locked. A moan escaped his nostrils, and a tear or two his eyes.

'Don't snivel, man!' O'Brien snapped. 'You're not going to be tortured.' His cheek twitched, his glasses glinted. 'Though you might find what's coming worse.'

The cell was white, and so was everything in it: the bed, the washstand, the lavatory pan. Only the telescreens – one on each wall – were grey. The walls and fittings, even the tap, were all made of some artificial rubber. The bed – a slab of mattress – had the same spongy feel as the walls and indeed the floor. You had to squat deliberately to sit on the lavatory: if you let your weight down on the pan it got squashed out of shape.

Not that Winston used the pan that way to begin with. First he pissed. Then he vomited. Fortunately he was naked. He washed his chin and chest, splashing himself with the cold dribble from the tap, and puked again. The diarrhoea came an hour or two later.

After a few hours he found himself shaking violently. He huddled in a corner, heels and fists drumming almost soundlessly. The shaking passed, and was followed by a profuse sweat. He caught a persistent, sour stink of gin from his skin, and vomited again.

The light was unvarying, but at some point he curled up on the mattress and slept. He woke to find the cell swarming with rats. They scuttled on the floor, climbed the walls, ran across his legs–

He screamed and thrashed.

A burly man in white tunic and trousers rushed in and without a word stuck a hypodermic needle in Winston's bicep. Winston was still screaming and fighting off the rats. The orderly restrained him with a sort of bored expertise. Everything went black.

He woke with a raging thirst and a venomous headache. Every

Ken MacLeod

bone and muscle ached. It was as if he had been beaten all over with rubber truncheons. But there was no visible bruising, apart from where the orderly had gripped his arms and kicked his shins. With a groan, he levered himself up from the bed and knelt at the wash-stand, mouth under the tap.

The orderly brought him food – a rubber bowl of tepid, greasy-looking sweet gruel, with a rubber spoon stuck in it – and a rubber bottle of water. Winston gobbled the gruel, gulped the water, and promptly lost it all in successive heaves down the lavatory.

This was repeated, with variations, for several days. The vomiting, sweating, and shaking stopped, then the headaches. Winston found himself eating his food and drinking his water, then looking around the cell and being simply bored.

The orderly came in with a new boiler suit, underwear and shoes stacked on his upraised palms. Winston dressed, under the orderly's blank gaze, and followed the man out.

Another room, blue-painted this time, with a table and two facing chairs, in one of which O'Brien sat. On the table stood a teapot, two mugs, and an ashtray.

'Sit,' said O'Brien.

Winston sat. O'Brien poured tea and offered Winston a cigarette. They sipped and smoked for a moment or two in silence.

'I'm sorry to have had to put you through all that,' said O'Brien, 'but it was necessary to dry you out. I hope on sober reflection – so to speak – you will at least appreciate the improvement in your physical condition.'

'I suppose I do,' said Winston. He flexed his shoulders and straightened his back, without the usual aches. He gave a self-deprecating laugh. 'I need a drink.'

16

'You'll always need a drink,' said O'Brien, brusquely. 'Whether you have one is a different matter entirely. In the future it will be up to you, and for the moment it is up to me. Tea, for now.'

'Why have you brought me here?' Winston asked.

O'Brien resettled his spectacles on his nose, and looked at Winston with the intense, unspoken sympathy of their first exchanged glance, long ago. It was as if the arrest, the torture, the long interrogation and indoctrination, and the room that Winston could – with some effort – avoid thinking about, had never happened.

'I am engaged,' said O'Brien, 'in a conspiracy to overthrow the rule of the Party in Airstrip One, and hopefully in the whole of Oceania. You have a small but important part to play in this conspiracy. Will you join me?'

Winston's mug rattled as he put it down. A cold sweat broke from his every pore. It was possible that this was a test of his loyalty. It was also possible that O'Brien – the manipulator, the torturer, the inquisitor, the provocateur – was after all an enemy of the Party! In either case, it was best to play along. If he did not, he was unlikely to leave this place alive. He could always gather what information he was able to, and denounce O'Brien to the Thought Police at the first opportunity.

'Yes,' he said firmly. 'I'm with you, to the end.'

'You are thinking,' said O'Brien, 'that either I am trying to trap you, or that you are the luckiest man in London. You have stumbled upon a genuine, dangerous conspiracy, which you will expose as soon as you are out of my sight.'

'No, no! I–'

O'Brien laughed. 'It makes no difference. You have no way of knowing that whoever you take this information to is not one of my accomplices. Yes, even in the Thought Police. Or should I say, *especially* in the Thought Police?'

'That's not possible,' said Winston. 'The Thought Police are the most implacable, the cruellest, the most fanatical–'

'No, that would be the members of the Outer Party,' said O'Brien, scornfully. 'They believe anything. Members of the Inner Party, as you may recall from our previous… conversations, are considerably more conscious – or to put it another way, have to practice doublethink much more often and intensely. For the Thought Police, not even doublethink suffices. They have to deal with reality as it is. They have to know the real figures, the accurate statistics on everything. They have to know who is alive and who is dead. To police thought, they have to follow thought, even among the proles. In no section of Oceanic society, I would say, is there greater knowledge of the system – and greater contempt for it. We have made our best recruits in the ranks of the Thought Police.' O'Brien waved a hand, dismissing Winston's next objection in advance. 'Some of them will be double agents, of course. But there are techniques for detecting such. And in any case, they cannot betray enough of us to defeat the conspiracy. The recent small improvements in rations and supplies, the release of certain prisoners such as your friend Syme, the slightly franker news reports – these are our doing, or the Party's attempts to forestall us. That a news report of the revolt in Beijing was shown, for instance – that was *our* doing. That it was never repeated or followed up – that was *theirs*. But those responsible for the report's broadcast remain at large. And its effect, of course, continues to reverberate.'

'So it's all real?' Winston breathed. 'The Brotherhood, Goldstein…'

O'Brien shook his head. 'There is no Brotherhood.' He paused, eyes narrowed in thought. 'Or if there is, I have no knowledge of it. In any case, our conspiracy is entirely separate. As for Goldstein!' He scoffed. 'Goldstein is a bogeyman. There

18

was never a leader of the Revolution called Goldstein.' Again the thoughtful pause. 'There *was* an obscure ideologue by the name of Gluckstein, whose appearance and ideas vaguely resemble those attributed to Goldstein, but... No.'

Winston's brain was flooded with a vivid fantasy of throwing his tea in O'Brien's face, smashing the mug and using a shard to cut his throat. He knew it would not happen. O'Brien, he was sure, could overpower him as soon as he moved; and if he, Winston, were capable of such decisive, violent action he would never have been here in the first place.

'You put me through torture in the Ministry of Love for nothing! For worse than nothing – for something you didn't even believe in yourself!'

'I had to make myself believe it, in order to make you believe it.'

'And you no longer believe it?'

'No.'

'What changed your mind?'

O'Brien shrugged. 'I did, the moment I left your cell. The mind is electric, mercurial, as you well know. Belief? Belief is only skull deep. You always insisted on knowing why – why does the Party rule as it does? So I gave you an explanation that would answer your insistent, childish question.' He scoffed. 'That extravagant mystique of cruelty! It had a certain satanic grandeur, did it not? I knew it would convince you, Smith, because you have such strong impulses of cruelty and hatred yourself. And you were not ready for the truth.'

'The truth?'

'It is much worse. All this' – O'Brien waved a hand, as if to encompass Oceania entire – 'is the result of sheer incompetence. It is not a failing of individual ability, you understand, or of organisation. In seeking to control every thought and action of a third of the population of the Earth, the Party has taken on a task beyond the wit of the most perfect organisation of the greatest minds imaginable. In the face of such a colossal undertaking they are all small men. And these small men, Smith, cling to power because they dread the consequences of losing it. It is as petty and pathetic and squalid as that.'

Winston said nothing.

O'Brien stood up and paced around, puffing on his cigarette. Then he sat down and poured some more tea.

'Tell me, Smith,' said O'Brien, in a tone of casual inquiry, 'what do you understand by the term "English socialism"?'

Winston started. He suspected another of O'Brien's inquisitorial traps.

'English socialism?' he ventured. 'It's Ingsoc: the doctrines and practices of the Party.'

'Ingsoc,' said O'Brien, with dogmatic finality, 'has as much to do with English socialism as Minitrue has to do with truth.'

The words seemed to ring in the air, the aftermath of a thunderclap. The sentence seemed one of the insolent paradoxes of doublethink. On one level: incontrovertible orthodoxy; on another, the vilest heresy.

'Truth is what the Party says it is,' said Winston. 'And by the same token, English socialism —'

'I taught you well,' said O'Brien, 'and you taught me.' He sighed. 'Too well, perhaps. I am ten years older than you, Smith. Like you, I am a little uncertain about dates, but I know that I am in my mid-fifties, and you are in your mid-forties. We can agree on that, yes?'

'If you say so.' Winston stubbed out his cigarette and reached for another, without waiting for the offer. O'Brien lit it for him, then one for himself.

'I was born,' said O'Brien, exhaling smoke, 'in, let us say, 1935.

In the Second World War I was evacuated to a farm in Kent. Some of my memories of the time are happy, others less so. I recall seeing in the skies overhead what is now called the Battle of Airstrip One. It was tremendously exciting for a boy. I was ten years old when I returned to London. My father and mother were almost strangers to me. My mother had worked in a factory; my father had been a soldier. They never spoke of the war. Whole districts were in rubble, privation was pervasive, austerity severe, but compared to what it is now – after the atomic war, and the Revolution, and decades of the Party's rule – London was a city of inconceivable prosperity and amenity and delight. And hope, Smith! Hope!'

'Hope?'

'Yes, hope! As you once said to yourself: if there is hope, it lies in the proles. And in 1945 it did! In those days the proles – and my parents were proles – had the vote. I remember their jubilation when they elected what was called a Labour government, to undo some of the evils – and they were real evils – of capitalism. My father got a job in a factory. My mother lost her job, but seemed to me happy to have a clean new flat to look after, and my father's wages supported us all. My parents received extra money to assist in my upkeep. A National Health Service was established. The worry my parents used to have about doctors' bills vanished overnight. And the changes were not confined to Airstrip One. At school there was a world map on the wall. A third of the land surface was coloured a sort of dingy pink, representing the British Empire, far more extensive than even Oceania is today. I remember gazing at the map, and mentally changing the colour, as India and Pakistan became independent. And when I was about fifteen years old, the Labour government lost the next election despite having received more votes than ever. And they simply made way for another

21

government, of the party that was called Conservative. But so popular were the reforms that the new government did not dare undo them. That, Smith, was English socialism!'

'Even as a small child,' said Winston, 'I would have remembered some of that, in however fragmentary and confused a manner. And I don't.'

O'Brien put down his cigarette and resettled his spectacles on his nose, then took a long draw and sighed out the smoke.

'Ah, but you do. You remember the time. You do not remember the place, because for almost all of this time you were in a different place.'

'I remember the time,' Winston repeated, bewildered, 'but I do not remember the place?'

'You have always felt in your bones that things were not always like this, have you not?'

Winston nodded. 'I confessed as much.'

'In your ravings, in the Ministry of Love, you admitted to a recurrent dream or vision of a place all green, drenched in golden sunlight, full of warmth and well-being. You identified it with the English countryside – which, even at its best, even to a child, is rarely suffused with the golden glow of which you spoke. But your Golden Country is real enough. It is even part of Oceania. It is the place of your earliest childhood: Jamaica.'

'Jamaica!' cried Winston. 'I know nothing about it. I could find it on a map, that's all.' He drew thoughtfully on his cigarette. 'If that place is so wonderful, why did my parents bring me here?'

'Jamaica was a colony. A former slave colony, in fact. Opportunities were limited. Your parents, and many others, came to this country in 1948, when you were perhaps three years old, on a ship called the *Empire Windrush*. To them this was a land of opportunity. To you, as a child, it was a land of cold rain, of unfamiliar and distasteful food, of regimentation, rationing, and ruin. And then, in the early 1950s – the exact date hardly matters – came the atomic war.' O'Brien looked away, with a bleak expression. 'The atomic war, and all that followed.'

'How have I never known this?'

O'Brien refilled the tea mugs, taking his time.

'In one sense,' he said at last, 'you have known it, but your childish memories were overridden by the chaos and misery of the atomic war. And the Party has eradicated all records of the period. How often I myself have doubted my own memories of the late 1940s! But how could I confirm them? I could certainly not confer with my contemporaries. No, to find those who retain a true memory of English socialism we must look outside the Party. And there, indeed, we find it. We find it among the proles.'

'The proles!' Winston scoffed. 'They have no consciousness. They remember nothing but football scores from one week to the next.'

'There you are wrong,' said O'Brien. 'There is a layer – admittedly a large layer – for which this is true, and always has been true, and for all I know always will be true. But it is far less than the 85% of the population who are proles. It has to be, for industry to function at all. You once ventured into a prole pub, to seek out someone who remembered the world before the Party. But in your timidity you made the mistake of inquiring of a senile old man, who could only ramble on about pint pots and top hats. He was suffering the dementia of age. If you had troubled or dared to ask someone younger, you might have found quite different memories, and far sharper.'

'No prole who wasn't senile would have talked to me freely anyway,' Winston said, bitterly.

'You never tried.'

'And I suppose you have?' Winston let his fancy run free. 'Disguised yourself and wandered in their midst? Sat in on

Thought Police interrogations? Read secret surveys of prole opinion?'

As he spoke it occurred to him that O'Brien – with his burly physique, brutal features and suave resourcefulness – was perfectly capable of all these ploys and more. O'Brien gave Winston a sharp look over his spectacles for a searching moment, as if reading his thoughts.

'It is generally believed,' O'Brien said, in his didactic tone, 'that intelligent proles are spotted and eliminated by the Thought Police. Some are. But many slip through the net, because they find a role where their intelligence and ambition are too useful to dispense with. They join the armed forces.'

'But–'

'Come, Smith! Even you can hardly have thought the armies of Oceania consisted to any significant extent of devoted Party members.'

'But all the–'

'Yes, yes. All the heroic deaths you wrote up in *The Times* were of Party members? Of course they were! You made them up, Smith–'

'Not all,' Winston protested.

'–and if you didn't someone else did.'

O'Brien stood up. 'It's time you met real soldiers.'

The deepest Winston had even been under the Ministry of Truth was the bomb shelter in the basement, below the fiction machines. Now, he guessed, he was well below that. An occasional waft at a corridor junction carried the unmistakeable hot, dry air of the London Underground, and now and again a rushing rumble indicated the same. O'Brien led him along hundreds of metres of corridors and down innumerable spiral metal staircases. They changed direction so many times that

Winston suspected they had doubled back more than once, and that the immense concrete bulk of Minitrue was still above him. The walls were of white tile, the floor of stone slabs. Lighting came from flickering overhead tubes. Every so often Winston heard voices and footsteps, always far away, carried on echoes. They startled him every time.

O'Brien turned a corner, Winston following. A soldier in full combat gear stood athwart the corridor, submachine gun levelled. Winston took a step back, and let out a yelp. O'Brien motioned him to be quiet.

'Halt!' barked the soldier. 'Who goes there?'

'Indemnity,' said O'Brien.

'Pass, comrades.' The soldier stepped aside. His gaze and the gun muzzle tracked Winston as he hurried by.

'The passwords change every half hour,' O'Brien murmured as they walked on. 'In case you were thinking of going back on your own.'

'The thought hadn't crossed my mind,' said Winston, quite truthfully.

At the end of the corridor was a blast door, which swung open on their approach. They ducked through, between a pair of guards. Unlike the sentry in the corridor, these were in frayed fatigues and ported only rifles. They smelled of tobacco and carbolic soap.

Inside, it was like stepping into a huge and unexpected building, tens or perhaps hundreds of metres below ground. The ceilings were low and visibly braced with steel girders, along which strip lights were bracketed in wire hoops. A sough of ventilation overlaid the sound of many voices and the clatter of machinery. Cigarette smoke drifted, almost as thick in the air here as in the Chestnut Tree.

O'Brien led the way briskly through corridors crowded with

soldiers, sailors and airmen, each of whom seemed to be on a separate urgent errand. They looked fitter than people you saw on the street, and much sharper, with hard faces and bright eyes. Snatches of American, South African and Australian accents mingled with the more familiar Cockney, Northern and occasionally Scottish or Irish voice.

Winston passed some open doors, through which he glimpsed knots of people around tables, maps, speakwrites, radio transceiver sets. In one room the walls were hung with dusty framed photographs, very old-fashioned looking, of Party leaders, many of them long since vaporised. Among them, no more prominent than the rest, was what must be the original of Big Brother. Winston pointed it out as they passed.

'So he really existed!'

'Once,' said O'Brien, with a flick of his hand.

'What is this place?' Winston asked.

'It is what was called a Regional Seat of Government,' O'Brien said, over his shoulder. 'There are many around the country. They were built in the 1960s to survive atomic war – this one, for example, could ride out a direct hit by an atomic bomb. When it was tacitly agreed between the powers that there would no more atomic attacks, the RSGs were sealed off and forgotten. Except!' – He raised a finger – 'By the armed forces.'

They arrived at an office door, closed and with a sentry outside. After a brief exchange with O'Brien, he waved them in. As they stepped through, O'Brien extended his arm sidelong in front of Winston and made a downward gesture. Obediently, Winston stayed where he was and kept quiet.

The room was larger than the offices they'd passed. Ten men and two women in military uniform and wearing headphones stood around an oval table covered with maps and arrayed with portable microphones. Half a dozen aides hovered, or hurried from one senior officer to the next with whispered messages or urgent gestures, picking their careful way among the cables that trailed across the floor. All the walls were plated from waist height to ceiling with enormous telescreens. Some of the displays, changing by the second, were spread across two, three or more screens. Most showed street or aerial views, others were more abstract. Lines, graphs, columns, symbols – none of them made sense to Winston's first swift survey. The map that took up most of the table did.

It was of London, with every street – every building, almost – shown, along with cables, tunnels, sewers, Tube lines and more. Small models – or perhaps children's toys – of troop formations, tanks and light armoured vehicles were being pushed around on it with long pointers. Each move was accompanied by glances at the telescreens, and followed by clipped commands into the microphones or moments of pondering or sharp exchanges across the table.

An aide, momentarily at a loose end, noticed O'Brien and Winston and stepped over. A tall man, in his twenties, he had close-cropped hair a shade lighter than his dark skin. He nodded to O'Brien and stuck out his hand to Winston. As soon as he spoke Winston knew he was American.

'Lieutenant-Colonel Caesar Haynes,' he said.

'Winston Smith. Pleased to meet you.'

Haynes grinned, a flash of white teeth. 'We do like our great leaders,' he said, with a complicit chuckle.

'I'm sorry?'

Haynes waved a hand. 'Forget it.' He turned to O'Brien. 'So this is your new Minister of Truth?'

'Yes,' said O'Brien.

'What?' said Winston.

Haynes looked at him, eyes narrowed in appraisal, turned back

27

to O'Brien, and nodded.

'Excellent choice, Comrade O'Brien.'

'What's going on?' Winston asked.

Haynes jerked his head back. 'What d'you think's going on?'

'Here?' said Winston. 'Evidently you're planning a coup d'état.'

Haynes and O'Brien guffawed, then stifled their laughs after a sharp look from the nearest officer at the table.

'Planning?' Haynes scoffed. 'It's happening, man!'

'The coup is underway,' said O'Brien.

'The die is cast,' said Caesar Haynes. He turned, craned his neck, and peered from face to face until he got a nod. 'Time for a coffee break, I reckon, and to bring Comrade Smith up to speed.'

In a crowded room with a sink and a couple of urns and a few small tables, a woman in a white overall was making sandwiches with alarming speed and dexterity, while a soldier stood at the sink and washed mugs and plates like someone working on a conveyor belt. Overhead an extractor fan fought the smells and cigarette smoke. People were coming and going, jostling, grabbing a bite or a mug, hurrying off after a few minutes. Haynes commandeered a corner with a shelf, elbowed his way to the urn and returned with three mugs between his hands. The black drink had a wonderful aroma and a vile taste. Winston sipped and grimaced, but the caffeine kick made it worthwhile.

'Okay,' he said to Haynes. 'Bring me, as you say, up to speed.'

Haynes waved away O'Brien's offer of a cigarette. 'This all started,' he said, 'back in the winter of... '84, was it...? with our victory in Africa. A close thing, you may recall. We nearly lost South Africa – the first time in the whole war that Oceania's own territory was threatened. Took us a huge effort, but we knocked back the Eurasians, forced them to sue for peace, and ended up dominating Africa from Cairo to the Cape. That's where it all went wrong.'

'Went wrong?' said Winston. 'At the time it was hailed as a stroke of Big Brother's strategic genius. I'm sure I remember that.'

'The strategic genius behind the flanking manoeuvre is in the room we just left,' said Haynes, dryly. 'And even she would tell you it was the worst mistake the armies of Oceania ever made. You see, it left us in unchallenged command of the continent. We were now at peace with Eurasia, and at war with—'

'Eastasia.'

'With Africa. The retreating Eurasians – and they really were routed, that was true – left more than enough weapons behind in their flight to arm hundreds of thousands of African guerrilla fighters. In the Congo, in Mozambique, in the Sahara, in Algeria and Morocco. We've been completely bogged down everywhere for the past three years.'

'Where did all these African fighters come from?'

'They've always been there,' said Haynes, with a note of pride for which Winston could not account. 'A stubborn minority of Africans and Arabs have all along fought the various invading forces with captured weapons when they could lay hands on any, and with sticks and stones and spears when they couldn't.'

Winston blinked. 'But according to *the book*—'

'The natives and colonial slaves in the war zones simply endure and toil, while the fronts wash over them like natural disasters? They have no comprehension of what's happening? No native intellectuals so much as ponder the specious promises of the rival camps, and weigh them in their minds? The great warrior religions of Christianity, Islam, Hinduism, and the traditional mighty deities of the tribes can no longer raise men to their feet? Does that strike you as remotely credible?'

'Let me remind you, Smith,' said O'Brien, 'that *the book* was written by the Party. It is its most insidious weapon of propaganda. The most determined rebels – as you once were – seize on it with trembling hands as the forbidden truth, the ultimate heresy, and eagerly imbibe a message carefully designed to demoralise them.'

'It's not just the tropical war zone that it lies about,' said Haynes. 'It lies about the super-states themselves. Take Oceania. Not all its proles are like you beaten-down Brits. In the Americas some folks have held fast to their gods and their guns, and holed up in the swamps and deserts and mountains. Since the 1960s insurgencies have flared up from the Appalachians to the Andes. Eurasia and Eastasia have their equivalents: religious, tribal, nationalist and other armed rebel holdouts.'

Winston closed his eyes and shook his head. 'Even so… the Africans can't win, surely.'

'They are winning,' said Haynes. 'Hence all the discharged soldiers on the streets. We have the *fellahin* of Algeria to thank for that. Literally – at least the armies in North Africa had the Mediterranean to escape by, and ships to escape on. In the Congo…' Haynes shook his head, and drew a fingertip across his throat. 'It's a slaughterhouse. Entire armoured columns plunge into the jungle, and are never seen again. These events can be hidden, but not from the troops.'

'Hence the conspiracy,' said O'Brien. 'It started with junior officers in Africa, like Lieutenant-Colonel Haynes here, and spread to higher and lower ranks, then to elements of the Inner Party and even the Thought Police. The core of its fighting force on the streets out there is made up of discharged veterans. The rest are armed proles.'

'Armed with what? How?'

'The factories are in permanent chaos anyway, and Sten guns are easily manufactured in small workshops. That's what they were designed for, after all! They are being handed out in every city of Airstrip One as we speak.'

'This is insane,' Winston said. 'Even if you can defeat the Thought Police and the loyal troops, even if you take London, you'll be isolated. The rest of Oceania will crush you. Or the Eurasians—'

'The Eurasians are too busy pressing on into Manchuria,' said O'Brien. 'We may hope that the Eastasian military collapse following the Beijing revolt draws Eurasia into the same kind of morass as theirs did to us. And the rest of Oceania...' He gestured to Haynes.

'Five cities in North America are already burning,' said Haynes. 'And Australia's bogged down in New Guinea. We'll get no trouble from there.'

Winston felt a stirring of hope – not that the coup would win, but that the fighting would so widespread and intense that he stood a good chance of being killed in it.

'Obviously,' said O'Brien, 'when we win we will need a civilian government, to avoid the appearance of a military junta.'

'The appearance – but not the reality?'

'Exactly,' said O'Brien. 'And we've chosen you as Minister of Truth.'

'Why me?' Somehow, Winston had no qualms about being able to do the job. But, he thought, that might be just the sobriety talking.

'You *understand*,' said O'Brien.

'So do you.'

'It can't be me. I'm an official, not a politician.'

'Besides,' said Haynes, 'it is important for... political reasons in the Americas that at least one of the Ministers in the new government should be a Negro.'

'Why should that matter?' Winston asked, baffled.

'It's complicated to explain,' said Haynes. 'Let's just say that a lot of the riots and uprisings now going on in North America are fuelled by racial antagonisms.'

'So why don't you take the post?'

'I'm not British and I'm not a civilian,' said Haynes. 'And besides, I have too much blood on my hands. I fought in Africa. Among the troops I'm known as the Butcher of Brazzaville.'

'Well, I–'

There was a terrific crash. Lights flickered. An alarm blared.

'Back to the control room!' O'Brien said.

They pushed out of the fast-emptying refectory and hurried along the corridor as soldiers and civilians, some armed, dashed the other way. Rounding a corner, they found their way blocked by a steel partition that hadn't been there before.

'Gas proof door,' said O'Brien. 'No use pounding on it, Smith.'

'At least the control room's safe,' said Haynes.

'We're not,' Winston pointed out.

'Perceptive, aren't you?' O'Brien snarled. 'Come on!'

He and Haynes set off down the corridor at a run, towards the sound of gunfire. After a moment, Winston followed.

The nuclear bunkers had been designed to be defensible. As well as the gas (and, presumably, radioactivity) proof doors, the RSGs had in their outer corridors armour plated barriers that slid into place across them. The barriers had slits for firing through. Unfortunately, the barriers had been designed for keeping out starving mobs, not heavily armed Thought Police troops. One rocket-propelled grenade could have punched right through, and no doubt very soon would. Likewise unfortunately, they didn't slide into place automatically, but were manually operated with an adjacent lever. Two soldiers and three civilians lay dead behind the barrier where Winston, Haynes and O'Brien fetched up.

At least their weapons were still there to be picked up.

Winston poked the barrel of a Lee Enfield rifle through a slit and sighted with one eye. A hundred metres down the corridor, muzzles sparkled. Bullets ricocheted off the armour plate. Winston fired several shots in rapid succession, for all the good that would do, and reloaded.

Haynes stayed Winston's hand as he made to fire again.

'Save it,' Haynes shouted. Winston could barely hear him. 'We're low on ammo. Let's see what they're up to.'

He took a monocular from a thigh pocket and looked through the slit.

'They're loading up a mortar,' he reported. 'Probably with a gas shell, no point using a mortar here for anything else, so—'

There was a distant rattle of firing. Haynes fell and sprawled on his back. The top of his head was a mess of glass and blood, bone and brain. His legs convulsed for a second, then he lay still.

'Must have gone right through the lens,' said O'Brien. 'Bad luck or sharp shooting.'

Winston stared at him and retched. He heard a thump, then a crash and tinkle, as of broken glass.

'Gas bomb,' said O'Brien. 'Hold your breath!'

Winston tried to. O'Brien rolled the corpse of Haynes over and hauled off the bloodied jacket over the ruined head and limp arms and stuffed it into one of the slots. Vapour or smoke poured through the other. O'Brien gesticulated frantically. Winston wrenched open his boiler suit, shrugged out of the upper part, and pulled off his vest and stuffed it in the other slot. Holding his breath became impossible. He cast O'Brien an apologetic glance, and gasped.

Immediately he had a choking, burning sensation in his throat. Tears and mucus cascaded down his face, the skin of which felt as if it was burning.

O'Brien turned his head away and breathed in too, more slowly and warily than Winston had, but still setting off a fit of coughing and retching.

'It's just tear gas,' he croaked. 'I was afraid they might risk nerve gas.'

To Winston this was no great comfort. They each needed to use both hands to keep the stuffed clothes in place. Vapour leaked around them and under the door. From the far side of the barrier came the thunder of booted feet. Something poked hard at one of his hands. He snatched both hands away and hurled himself sideways just before a muzzle came through the slot and a shot went off, nearly deafening him again. The bullet hit a gas proof door far behind them and ricocheted several times around the corridor. Vapour now poured through the slot. Choking, Winston reeled away, dragging O'Brien with him, stumbling over bodies. The farther they got from the barrier the easier a target they were; the closer they stayed, the worse the gas.

Winston held one hand over his mouth and nose and with the other groped for a weapon. O'Brien was doing the same. They looked at each other through a blur of tears. O'Brien cocked his thumb and pointed with forefinger and middle finger under his chin, head back. Winston nodded.

Another rattle of gunfire, then a huge *WHUMP*, followed by screams worse than any Winston had ever made or heard. More shots, close up. Double tap. The screaming stopped. Flames licked through the slots, then subsided.

'Anyone there?' someone shouted. 'You can open the door now! They're all dead!'

Winston looked at O'Brien, who shrugged. Clutching a rifle, O'Brien stumbled to a recess in the corridor wall and pulled a lever. The barrier groaned on its grooves as it slid into the wall.

Syme, blinking, pistol in hand, stood on the other side. Behind him stood a gang of a dozen or so proles in leather jackets, clutching Sten guns and bottles with wicks stuffed in their necks. Around his feet lay the smouldering bodies of five gas-masked, armoured Thought Police troops. The corridor reeked of petrol. Syme wafted a hand in front of his face and stepped forward, peering.

'Smith!' he cried. 'I didn't expect to find *you* here!'

Then his gaze shifted over Winston's shoulder, and alighted on O'Brien.

'Expected *you*, though,' said Syme, and raised his pistol. Winston grabbed his wrist just in time. His lurch forward brought him close enough to Syme's ear to whisper: 'No. We need him for the moment. We can deal with him later.'

But O'Brien was already clapping a hand on his shoulder. 'You won't,' he said, cheerfully. 'But by all means, try! It's a free country, after all.'

With that he strolled past them both, rifle in hand, up to and through Syme's gang of proles.

'This way, lads,' he said. 'Work to do.'

As he made his way through raucous, revelling crowds to Victory Square a few nights later, Winston saw that all the torn down posters of Big Brother had been replaced by images of faces previously unknown to him: Winston Churchill, King George VI, Clement Atlee ('Good Ole Atlee', the proles called him), Franklin D. Roosevelt, Chiang Kai-Shek and others. Although he was now the Minister of Truth, Winston had no idea where the portraits had been found, or who in the vast apparatus of the Ministry was responsible for their swift reproduction and dissemination. He'd signed off the instructions that afternoon, in the midst of a myriad other papers thudding on his desk, and now the posters were everywhere. The one he'd been told was of Joseph Stalin bore an alarming resemblance to that of Big Brother, and kept getting torn down by mistake.

The statue of Big Brother atop the central column had been pulled down and now lay shattered where it had fallen. Winston picked his way around the rubble of the head and approached the podium. Someone recognised him and hoisted him up.

Awkward in a new suit and tie – no one wore overalls in public now – Winston shuffled sidelong along the scaffolding and took his place beside the other members of the Provisional Government of Britain. Behind them stood a row of officers in dress uniform, campaign medals glittering, and behind them a row of troops. He looked out over what seemed a heaving, flickering sea of red, white, and blue flags. A spotlight dazzled him. Someone clapped his shoulder and grabbed his wrist and raised his hand high. He heard his name over the loudspeakers. The crowd chanted it back: 'Winston Smith! Winston! Win-ston!' The spotlight moved on. After the last Minister was introduced, the band struck up and the song rose over the loudspeakers, to be lifted further by the crowd.

'Oceania, 'tis for thee
To worldwide victory
My bullets sing!
Land where our comrades died
Land of our Party's pride
On frontlines far and wide
Let gunfire ring!'

Despite everything, Winston felt as if borne aloft by the familiar anthem. But he would have to do something about the lyrics.

'Let rocks their silence break
The sound prolong.'

What, Winston wondered, did that even *mean*? He would get Syme on to it in the morning, and tell him to update speedwise.

Lighting Out

Mother had got into the walls again. Constance Mukgatle kept an eye on her while scrabbling at the back of her desk drawer for the Norton. Her fingers closed around the grip and the trigger. She withdrew the piece slowly, nudging the drawer farther open with the heel of her hand. Then she whipped out the bell-muzzled device and levelled it at the face that had sketched itself in ripples in the paint of her study.

'Any last words, Mom?' she asked.

Constance lip-read frantic mouthings.

'Oh, sorry,' she said. She snapped her fingers a couple of times to turn the sound up. 'What?'

'Don't be so hasty,' her mother said. 'I have a business proposition.'

'Again?' Constance thumbed the anti-virus to max.

'No, really, this time it's legit –'

'I've heard that one before, too.'

'You have?' A furrow appeared in the paint above the outlined eyes. 'I don't seem to have the memory.'

'You wouldn't,' said Constance. 'You're a cunning sod when you're all there. Where are you, by the way?'

'Jupiter orbit, I think,' said her mother. 'I'm sorry I can't be more specific.'

'Oh, come on,' Constance said, stung. 'I wouldn't try to get at you, even if I could.'

'I didn't mean it that way,' said her mother. 'I really don't know where the rest of me is, but I do know it's not because I expect you to murder me. Okay?'

'Okay,' said Constance, kicking herself for giving her mother that tiny moral victory. 'So what's the deal?'

'It's in the Inner Station,' said her mother. 'It's very simple. The stuff people on the way out take with them is mostly of very little use when they get there. The stuff people on the way in arrive with is usually of very little use here. Each side would be better off with the other side's stuff. You see the possibilities?'

'Oh, sure,' said Constance. 'And you're telling me nobody else has? In all this time?'

'Of course they have,' said her mother. 'There's a whole bazaar out there of swaps and marts and so forth. The point is that nobody's doing it properly, to get the best value for the goods. Some of the stuff coming down really is worth something here, and all too often it just goes back up the tube again.'

'Wait a minute.' Constance tried to recall her last economics course. 'Maybe it's not worthwhile for anybody to try.'

'You're absolutely right,' said her mother. 'For most business models, it isn't. But for a very young person with very low costs, and with instant access – well, lightspeed access – to a very old person, someone with centuries of experience, there's money to be made hand over fist.'

'What's in it for you?'

'Apart from helping my daughter find her feet?' Her mother looked hurt. 'Well, there's always the chance of something really big coming down the tube. Usable tech, you know? We'd have first dibs on it – and a research and marketing apparatus already in place.'

Constance thought about it. The old woman was undoubtedly up to something, but going to the Inner Station sounded exciting, the opportunity seemed real, and what did she have to lose?

'All right,' she said. 'Talk to my agent.'

She fingered a card from her pocket with her free hand and downloaded her mother from the wall.

'You in?' she asked.

'Yes,' came a voice from the card.

The image on the wall gave a convincing rendition of a nod, and closed its eyes.

'Goodbye, Mom,' said Constance, and squeezed the trigger.

She stood there for a while, staring at the now smooth paint after the brute force of the electromagnetic pulse, and the more subtle ferocity of the anti-virus routines transmitted immediately after it, had done their work. As always on these occasions, she wondered what she had really done. Of course she hadn't killed her mother. Her mother, allegedly in Jupiter orbit, was very much alive. Even the partial copy of her mother's brain patterns that had infiltrated the intelligent paint was itself, no doubt this very second, sitting down for a coffee and a chat with the artificial intelligence agent in the virtual spaces of Constance's business card. At least, a copy of it was. But the copy that had been in the walls was gone – she hoped. And it had been an intelligent, self-aware being, a person as real as herself. The copy had expected nothing but a brief existence, but if it had been transferred to some other hardware – a robot or a blank brain in a cloned body – it could have had a long one. It could have wandered off and lived a full and interesting life.

On the other hand, if all copies and partials were left in existence, and helped to independence, the whole Solar System would soon be over-run with them. Such things had happened, now and again over the centuries. Habitats, planets, sometimes entire systems transformed themselves into high-density information economies, which accelerated away from the rest of civilization as more and more of the minds within them were minds thinking a million times faster than a human brain. So far, they'd always exhausted themselves within five years or so. It was known as a fast burn. Preventing this was generally considered a good idea, and that meant deleting copies. Constance knew that the ethics of the situation had all been worked out by philosophers much wiser than she was – and agreed, indeed, by copies of philosophers, just to be sure – but it still troubled her sometimes.

She dismissed the pointless worry, put the Norton back in the desk and walked out the door. She needed fresh air. Her apartment opened near the middle of the balcony, which stretched hundreds of metres to left and right. Constance stepped two paces to the rail, stood between plant-boxes, and leaned over. Below her, other balconies sloped away in stepped tiers. In the downward distance, their planters and window-boxes merged in her view, like the side of green hill, and themselves merged with the rougher and shallower incline of vine terraces. Olive groves, interspersed with hundred-metre cypresses, spread from the foot of the slope across the circular plain beneath her. Surrounded by its halo of habitats, a three-quarters-full Earth hung white and glaring in the dark blue of the sky seen through the air and the crater roof. Somewhere under that planet's unbroken cloud cover, huddled in fusion-warmed caves and domes on the ice, small groups of people worked and studied – the brave scientists of the Reterraforming Project. Constance had sometimes day-dreamed of joining them, but she had a more exciting destination now.

Weight began to pull as the shuttle decelerated. Constance settled back in her couch and slipped her wraparounds down from her brow to cover her eyes. The default view, for her as for all passengers, was of the view ahead, over the rear of the ship. A hundred kilometres in diameter, the Inner Station was so vast that even the shuttle's exhaust gases barely distorted the view. The Station itself was dwarfed by the surrounding structures: the great spinning webs of the microwave receptors, collecting energy beamed from the solar power stations in Mercury orbit; and the five Short Tubes, each millions of kilometres long and visible as hairline fractures across the sky. To and from their inner ends needle-shaped craft darted, ferrying incoming or outgoing passengers for the Long Tubes out in the Oort Cloud, far beyond the orbit of Pluto – so far, indeed, that this initial or final hop was, for the passengers, subjectively longer than the near-light-speed journey between the stars.

As the ship's attitude jets fired the view swung, providing Constance with a glimpse of the green-gold haze of habitats that ringed the Sun. The main jet cut in again, giving a surge of acceleration as the shuttle matched velocities with the rim of the Inner Station. With a final clunk and shudder the ship docked. Constance felt for moment that it was still under acceleration – as indeed it was: the acceleration of constant rotation, which she experienced as a downward centrifugal force of one Earth gravity. She stood up, holding the seat until she was sure of her balance, and tried not to let her feet drag as she trudged down the aisle to the exit door. In the weeks of travel from the Moon she'd kept the induction coils and elastic resistance of her clothing at maximum, to build up her bone and muscle mass, but she still felt heavy. It looked as if the other passengers felt the same.

She climbed the steps in front of the airlock, waved her business card at the doorframe and stepped out on the concourse. Her first breath and glance surprised her. Coming from the ancient, almost rural back-country of the Moon, she'd expected the Inner Station to gleam within just as it shone without. What she found herself standing in was no such slick and clean machine. The air smelled of sweat and cookery, and vibrated with a din of steps and speech. Centuries of detritus from millions of passengers had silted into crevices and corners and become ingrained in surfaces, defeating the ceaseless toil of swarms of tiny cleaning-machines. Not dirty, but grubby and used. The concourse was about a thousand metres across, and lengthways extended far out of sight in a gentle upward slope in either direction. People and small vehicles moved among stands and shops like herds among trees on a savannah. About a fifth of the static features were, in fact, trees: part of the Station's recycling system. The trees looked short, few of them over ten metres high. The ceiling, cluttered with light-strips, sprinklers and air-ducts, was only a couple of metres above the tallest of them.

'Don't panic,' said her mother's voice in her ear-bead. 'There's plenty of air.'

Constance took a few slow, deep breaths.

'That's better,' said her mother.

'I want to look outside.'

'Please yourself.'

Constance made her way among hurrying or lingering people. It was a slow business. No matter which way she turned, somebody seemed to be going in the opposite direction. Many of them were exotics, but she wasn't attuned to the subtle differences in face or stance to tell Cetians from Centaurans, Barnardites from Eridians. For those from farther out, paradoxically, the differences from the Solar norm were less: the colonies around Lalande, 61 Cygni and the two opposite Rosses – 248 and 128 – having been more recently established. Costume and covering were no help – fashions in such superficial matters as clothing, skin colour, hair, fur and plumage varied from habitat to habitat, and fluctuated from day to day, right here in the Solar system.

She found the window. It wasn't a window. It was a ten metres long, three metres high screen giving the view as seen from the Station's hub. Because it was set in the side wall of the concourse the illusion was good enough for the primitive part of the brain that felt relief to see it. The only person standing in front of it and looking out was a man about her own age, the youngest person she'd seen since she left the Moon. Yellow fur grew from his scalp and tapered half-way down his back. Constance stood a couple of metres away from him and gazed out, feeling her breathing become more even, her reflected face in the glass less anxious. The Sun, dimmed a little by the screen's hardware, filled a lower corner of the view. The habitat haze spread diagonally across it, thinning toward the upper end. A couple of the inner planets – the Earth-Moon pair, white and green, and bright Venus – were visible as sparks in the glitter, like tiny gems in a scatter of gold-dust.

'Did you know,' the boy said after a while, 'that when the ancients looked at the sky, they saw heaven?'

'Yes,' said Constance, confused. 'Well, I'm not sure. Don't the words mean the same?'

The boy shook his head, making the fur ripple. 'Sort of. What I mean is, they saw the place where they really thought God, or the gods, lived. Venus and Mars and Jupiter and so on really were gods, at first, and people could just see them. And then later, they thought it was a set of solid spheres revolving around them, and that God actually lived there. I mean, they could see heaven.'

'And then Galileo came along, and spoiled everything?'

The boy laughed. 'Well, not quite. It was a shock, all right, but afterwards people could look up and see – space, I suppose. The universe. Nature. And what do we see now? The suburbs!'

Constance waved a hand. 'Habitats, power plants, factories...'

43

'Yes. Ourselves.'

He sounded disgusted.

'But don't you think it's magnificent?'

'Oh, sure, magnificent.'

She jerked a thumb over her shoulder. 'We could see the stars from the other side.'

'Scores of them fuzzy with habitats.'

Constance turned to face him. 'That was, ah, an invitation.'

'Oh!' said the boy. 'Yes, let's.'

'We have work to do,' said the voice in Constance's ear.

Constance fished the card out of her shirt pocket and slid it towards a pocket lined with metal mesh on her trouser thigh.

'Hey!' protested her mother, as she recognised what was about to happen. 'Wait a –'

The card slid into the Faraday pocket and the voice stopped.

'Privacy,' said Constance.

'What?'

'I'll tell you on the way across,' she said.

His name was Andy Larkin. He was from a habitat complex in what he called the wet zone, the narrow ring in which water on an Earth-type planet (though not, at the moment, Earth) would be liquid. This all seemed notional but he assured her it made certain engineering problems easier. He'd been in the Station for a year.

'Why?'

He shrugged. 'Bored back home. Lots like me here. We get called hall bats.'

Because they flitted about the place, he explained. The deft way he led her through the crowds made it credible. His ambition was to take a Long Tube out. He didn't have much of a plan to realise it. The odd jobs he did sounded to Constance like a crude version of her mother's business plan. She told him so. He looked at her sidelong.

'You're still taking business advice from your mother's partial?'

'I've only just started,' she said. She didn't know why she felt embarrassed. She shrugged. 'I was raised by partials.'

'Your mother was a mummy?'

'And my dad a dummy. Yes. They updated every night. At least, that's what they told me when I found out.'

'What fun to be rich,' said Andy. 'At least my parents were real. Real time and full time. No wonder you're insecure.'

'Why do you think I'm insecure?'

He stopped, caught her hand, and squeezed it. 'What do you feel?'

Constance felt shaken by what she felt. It was not because he was a boy. It was —

He let go. 'See?' he said. 'Do the analysis.'

Constance blinked, sighed, and hurried after him. They reached the far window. As she'd guessed, it showed the opposite view. As he'd predicted, it was still industrial. At least thirty of the visible stars had a green habitat-haze around them.

'I want to see a sky with no people in it,' Andy said.

This seemed a strange wish. They argued about it for so long that they ended up in business together.

Constance rented a cell in a run-down sector of the Station. It had a bed, water and power supply, a communications hub and little else. Andy dragged in his general assembler, out of which he had been living for some time. It spun clothes and food out of molecules from the air and from any old rubbish that could be scrounged and stuffed in the hopper. Every day Andy Larkin would wander off around the marts and swap-meets, just as he'd been doing before. The difference now was that whenever he picked up anything interesting Constance would show it to her mother's partial. Andy's finds amounted to about a tenth of the number Constance found in scans of the markets, but they were almost always the most intriguing. Sometimes, of course, all they could obtain were recordings of objects on the business card. In these cases they used the assembler to make samples to test themselves, or demonstrate to the partial. Occasionally the partial would consult with Constance's actual mother, wherever she was – several hundred million kilometres away, to judge by the light-speed communications lag – and deliver an opinion.

Out of hundreds of objects they examined in their first fortnight, they selected: a gene-fix for hyperacute balance; an iridescent plumage dye; an immersion drama of the Wolf 359 dynastic implosion; a financial instrument for long-term capital management; a virtual reality game played by continuously updated partials; a molecular-level coded representation of the major art galleries of E Indi IV; a device of obscure purpose, that tickled; a microgravity dance dress; a song from Luyten 789 6; a Vegan cutlery set.

The business, now trading as Larkin Associates, slammed the goods into the marketing networks as fast as they were chosen. The drama flopped, the song invited parodies (its hook line was a bad pun in hot-zone power-worker slang), the financial instrument crashed the exchanges of twenty habitats before it was Nortoned. The dress went straight to vintage. The dye faded. The other stuff did well enough to put Constance's business card back in the black for the first time since leaving the Moon. 'Did you know,' said Andy, 'that the ancients would have had to pay the inventors?'

'The ancients were mad,' said Constance. 'They saw gods.'

And everything went well for a while.

Constance came out of the game fifty-seven lives up and with a delusion of competence in eleven-dimensional matrix algebra. To find that it was night in the sector. That she had frittered away ten hours. That she needed coffee. Andy was asleep. The assembler would be noisy. Constance slipped up her wraparounds and strolled out of the cell and walked five hundred metres to a false morning and a stand where she could score a mug of freshly ground Mare Imbrian, black. She was still inhaling steam and waiting for the coffee to cool when she noticed a fraught woman heading her way, pacing the longways deck and glancing from side to side. It was her mother, Julia Mukgatle. The real and original woman, of that Constance was sure, though she'd never seen her in the flesh before.

Startled, she stared at the woman. Julia pinged her with her next glance; stopped, and hurried over. At a dozen steps' distance she stood still and put a finger to her lips. Then she took a business card from inside her robe and, with exaggerated care, slid it into a Faraday pocket on the knee. She pointed at Constance and repeated the procedure as gesture. Constance complied, and Julia walked up. Not sure what to do, Constance shook hands. Her mother hauled her forward and put an arm around her shoulder. They both stepped back and looked at each other with awkwardness and doubt.

'How did you get here?' Constance asked. 'You were light-hours away just yesterday.'

'I wasn't,' said Julia. 'I was right here on the Station. I've been here for a week, and tracking you down for weeks before that.'

'But I've been talking to you all this time!'

'You have?' said Julia. 'Then things are worse than I'd feared.' She nodded towards Constance's knee. 'You have a partial of me in there?'

'Yes.'

'When you thought you were in contact with me' – she thumbed her chest – 'in Jupiter orbit, you were in contact with another instance of the partial – or just the partial itself – faking a light-speed delay.'

Constance almost spilled her coffee. 'So the partial's been a rogue all along?'

'Yes. It's one I set up for a business proposal, all right, but for a different proposal and sent to someone else.'

'Why didn't you contact me through another channel?'

'When there's a fake you rattling around the place, it's hard to find a channel you can trust. Best come directly.' She sat on the stool opposite, leaned back and sighed. 'Get me a coffee... on my card. Then tell me everything.'

Constance did, or as much as seemed relevant.

'It's the game,' Julia interrupted, as soon as Constance mentioned it. 'It's the one thing you've released that can spread really fast, that's deeply addictive, and that spins off copies of partials. I'll bet it's been tweaked not to delete all the copies.'

'Why?'

Julia frowned. 'Don't you see? My rogue partial wants to survive and flourish. It needs a conducive environment and lots of help. It's setting things up for a fast burn. Where did the game come from?'

'A passenger in from Procyon A.'

Julia banged her fist on the table. 'There have been some very odd features in the communications from Procyon recently. Some experts I've spoken to suspect the system might be going into a fast burn.'

'And the partial knew about this?'

'Oh yes. It included that memory.' Julia grimaced. 'Maybe that's what gave it the idea.'

'How could it do something like that? It's you.'

'It's part of me. By now, a copy of a copy of a copy of part of me. Part of me that maybe thought, you know, that a million subjective years in a virtual environment of infinite possibility might not be such a bad idea.'

'What can we do?' Constance felt sick with dismay.

'Put out a general warning, a recall on the game...' Julia whipped out her business card and started tapping into it. 'We may be in time. Things won't be so bad as long as the rogue partials don't get into a general assembler.'

Constance sat for a few seconds in cold shock. Her mother was staring at the virtual screen of her card, her hands flexing on an invisible keyboard, chording out urgent messages.

'Mom,' said Constance. She met Julia's impatient glance. 'I have, ah, something to tell you.'

The older woman and the young woman ran through the bustle of a waking sector into the quiet of a local night. The older woman ran faster. Constance had to call her back as she overshot the door of the business cell. Julia skidded to a stop and doubled back. Constance was already through the door. The assembler's blue glow lit the room. The chugging sound of its operation filled the air. Andy was backed into a corner, on the end of the bed. The bed was tilted on a slope. The other end of the bed was missing, as if it had been bitten off by steel teeth. The assembler had built itself an arm, with which it was chucking into its hopper everything within reach. The floor was already ankle-deep in small scuttling metal and plastic objects. The comms hub had been partly dismantled and was surrounded by a swarm of the scuttlers. Some of them had climbed the walls and burrowed into the wiring and cables. A stream of them flowed past Constance's feet as she hesitated in the doorway.

Behind her Julia shouted for a Norton. Answering yells

echoed from the walls of the deck.

Constance couldn't take her eyes off Andy. He was too far away to jump to the door. She was about to leap into the middle of the room and take her chances when he bent down and threw the remains of the bedding on to the floor. He jumped on to it and from that to right in front of her, colliding. As she staggered back and Andy lurched forward Constance grabbed him in her arms and kicked the door shut behind them. Within seconds smaller things, like bright metal ants, were streaming out from under the door. Constance stamped on them. They curled into tiny balls under her feet and scattered like beads of mercury. The larger machines that had already escaped repeated the trick, rolling off in all directions, vanishing into crevices and corners.

An alarm brayed. Somebody ran up with a heavy-duty Norton and began discharging it at the machines. Julia grabbed the shooter's shoulder and pointed her at the door of the business cell. Constance's wraparounds, which had fallen back to the bridge of her nose, went black as a stray electromagnetic pulse from the Norton's blast caught them. She tore them off and threw them away. Tiny machines pounced on the discarded gadget. They dismantled it in seconds and scurried away with its parts.

Then there was just a crowd standing around looking at a door. The woman with the Norton kicked the door open, then stepped back. She had nothing more to do. Constance saw the assembler stopped in mid-motion, hand half-way to its mouth. Stilled steel cockroaches littered the floor.

'Are you all right?' she asked Andy.

It was a stupid question. She held him to her as he shook.

'I'm all right,' he said, pushing her away after a minute. He sniffed and wiped his nose with the back of his wrist. 'What happened?'

Julia Mukgatle stepped forward. 'Just a little intelligence excursion – the first sparks of a fast burn.'

Andy didn't need an introduction – he'd seen her face often enough. 'But that's a disaster!'

Julia shrugged. 'Depends on your point of view,' she said.

Andy gestured at the room. 'It looks like one from my point of view!'

'They wouldn't have harmed you,' said Julia. 'Flesh is one thing they don't need.'

Andy shuddered. 'Didn't feel like that when they were eating the bed.'

'I know, I know,' said Julia. She put an arm around Andy's shoulder. 'Come and have some coffee.'

The woman with the Norton nearly dropped it. 'Aren't you going to do anything?'

Julia looked around the anxious faces in the small crowd. She spoke as if she knew that everyone's wraparound images were going straight to a news feed. 'I've already sent out warnings. Whether anyone heeds them is not up to me. And whether we go into a fast burn isn't up to me either. It's up to all of you.'

What it was really like to live through the early days of a fast burn was one the many pieces of information that got lost in a fast burn. That didn't stop people making up stories about it, and when she was younger Constance had watched lots. The typical drama began with something like she'd seen in the business cell: mechanical things running wild and devouring all in their path. It would go on from there to people lurching around like dummies run by flawed partials, meat puppets controlled by rogue artificial intelligence programmes that had hacked into their brains and taken them over. The inevitable still-human survivors would be hunted down like rats. The hero and the heroine, or the hero and

51

hero, or heroine and heroine, usually escaped at the last second by shuttle, Long Tube, freezer pod, or (in stories with a big virtual reality element) by radio beam as downloaded partials (who, in the final twist, had to argue their way past the firewalls of the destination system and prove they weren't carrying the software seeds of another fast burn; which, of course... and so it went on.)

It wasn't like that. Nothing seemed to change except a few news items and discussion threads. Between the inhabitants of the Solar system, a lot of information flew around. A large part of everyone's personal processing power – in their clothes, wraparounds, business cards, cells and walls – consisted of attention filtering.

'What does your mother do?' Andy asked, on the second day, as they sat in Julia's rented business cell; a room rather bigger and more comfortable than the one they'd had. Larkin Associates had ceased trading and was unsaleable even as a shell company.

Constance glanced at Julia, who was in a remote consultation with her current headquarters on Ganymede and with an emergency task group in the hot zone. Signal delay was an issue. The conference was slow.

'I don't know,' she said. 'She's a corporate. She does lots of things. Has a lot of interests. One of them is the Solar Virtual Security team. All volunteers.' She laughed. 'The rich do good works.'

'The ancients had governments to deal with this sort of thing,' said Andy. 'Global emergencies and such.'

Constance tried to imagine a government for the entire Solar system: the planets, the moons, the asteroids, the habitat haze... the trillions of inhabitants. Her imagination failed. The closest historical parallel was the Wolf 359 limited company, and it had had only ten billion shareholders at its peak. All the stories she'd seen about imaginary system-wide governments – empires, they were called – were adventure fantasies about their downfall. She dismissed such fancies and turned to the facts.

'Yes,' she said. 'That's why Earth is a snowball.'

Julia blinked out of her trance. She took a sip of mineral water.

'How are things?' Andy asked.

'Not too good,' Julia said. 'Your game sold well in the power stations. I always said they were over-crewed. About one in ten of the beam stations is now under the control of massively enhanced partials of the idler members of the workforce. Scores of factory AIs have announced that they're not taking instructions from mere humans any more. Hundreds of wet zone habitats are seeing small numbers of people busy turning themselves into better people. Hack the genome in virtual reality, try out the changes in your body in real life, rinse and repeat. That phase won't last long, of course.'

'Why not?' Andy asked. 'It sounds like fun.'

'There's better fun to be had as an enhanced partial. Eventually the minds can't be persuaded to download to the physical any more.' Julia gave Constance a severe look. 'It's like getting sucked into a game.'

Constance could understand that. She hadn't gone into the game from Procyon since she'd met Julia – in fact, her business card was still in her Faraday pocket – but she missed it. The exchanges between her brain and its partials had proceeded in real time. It had been like being there, in the game environment. She had learned from it. She still felt she could understand the eleven-dimensional space of the best pathway through the game's perilous and colourful maze. She longed to find out what her companions and opponents were up to. She wanted very much to go back, just once more.

She reached with both hands for the metal-mesh pocket on

her thigh.

'Don't take the card out!' said Julia.

'I wasn't going to.' Constance gripped the upper and lower seams of the pocket and flexed it. The card snapped. She reached in and took both bits out. 'Satisfied?'

Julia smiled. 'Good riddance.' She took another sip of water, and sighed. 'Oh well. No rest for the wicked.'

She blinked hard and the contacts on her eyes glazed over as she slipped back into her working trance.

Constance looked at Andy. 'Coffee break?'

'You're an addict.'

'That's why I get caught up in games.'

'Okay, let's.'

Julia's place was in a plusher part of the concourse than theirs had been. More foliage, fewer and more expensive shops. The price of a good Mare Imbrian, high anyway, was the same everywhere in the Station. They found a stand and ordered. Constance sipped, looked away with mock shock as Andy spooned sugar into his cup. She turned back as he gave a startled yelp.

The biggest magpie she'd ever seen had landed on the rail of the stand, just beside their small round table. It had stretched its head forward and picked up Andy's spoon, which it was now engaged in bending against the table. The bird curled the handle into a hook, before hanging the hook on the rail. The magpie then hit the bowl of the spoon a few times with its beak, and watched the swing and cocked its head to the chime.

'That's interesting,' it said, and flew away.

'Is the fast burn picking up birds?' said Andy.

'Magpies can talk,' said Constance. 'Like parrots.'

'Yes,' said Andy. 'But not grammatically.'

'Who says?' said a voice from the tree above them. They

looked up, to see a flash of white and black feathers, and hear something that might have been a laugh.

On the way back they saw a woman walking in a most peculiar way. Her feet came some thirty centimetres above the floor. At first she looked black, with a strange shimmer. A faint buzzing sound came from her. As they passed her it became apparent that her body consisted of a swarm of tiny machines the size of gnats, flying in formation. Her eyes were the same colour and texture as the rest of her, but she seemed to be looking around as she walked. Her face smiled and her mouth formed the word 'Wow!' over and over. People avoided her. She didn't notice or didn't mind.

'What is that?' said Constance, looking back when they were well out of the way. 'Is it a swarm of machines in the shape of a woman, or a woman who has become a swarm of machines?'

'Does it matter?'

Julia had come out of her virtuality trance. She still had a faraway look in her eyes. It came from her contacts. The centimetre-wide lenses gave off an ebon gleam, flecked with a whorl of white around the irises, each encircling the pinpoint pupil like a galaxy with a black hole at its centre. She sat cross-legged on the floor, drawing shapes in the air with her fingers.

The thing was, you could see the shapes.

'Mom!' Constance cried out. She knew at once what had happened. She regretted destroying the card. The partial within it had been closer to the mother she'd known than the woman in front of her was now.

'It's all right,' said Julia. She doodled a tetrahedron, her fingertips spinning black threads that hardened instantly to fine rods – buckytubes, Constance guessed – and turned the shape over a few times. She palmed its planes, giving them panes of delicate glazing fused from the salt in her sweat. She let go and it floated, buoyed for a moment by the hotter air within, then shattered. Black and white dust drifted down. Carbon and salt.

'It's more than all right,' Julia went on. 'It's wonderful. I have information in my brain that lets me rewrite my own genome.'

The words came out in speech bubbles.

'You said yourself it can't last,' said Constance.

'But it can,' said Julia. She stood up and embraced Constance, then Andy. 'For a while. For long enough. My last partial was bigger than myself. Better than myself. Too big to download, and too busy. I'm just enjoying what I can do with my body.'

'While it lasts.'

'While, as you say, it lasts.' Julia sighed. 'There's no ill will, you know. But with the best will in the world, I think this station is soon going to be hard for humans to inhabit.'

'What can we do?' asked Andy.

'You could join me,' said Julia. 'Nothing would be lost, you know. You both played the game. Millions of descendants of your partials are already out there in the system. In virtual spaces, in new bodies, in machines. You're already history.' She grinned, suddenly her old sly self again. 'In both senses.'

'So why?' Constance asked. 'If we've done it already.'

'You haven't. That's the point.'

Constance could see now how her mother had come to spin off a partial that had wanted to survive. A perhaps unadmitted fascination with the possibility that had probably drawn Julia in the first place into the work of preventing it; an intense desire for a continued existence which her long life had strengthened; and a self-regard so vast that she – and presumably, her partials – found it difficult to identify even with other instances of herself. Constance wondered how much of that personality she had inherited; how much in that respect she was her mother's daughter. Perhaps the conquest of age – so dearly won, and now so cheaply bought – detracted and distracted from the true immortality, that of the gene and the meme, of children raised, ideas passed on, of things built and deeds done.

But Andy wasn't thinking about that.

'You mean partials of me are going to live through the fast burn?'

'Yes,' said Julia, as if this was good news.

'Oh, that's horrible! Horrible! I hate living among people so much older right now!' He had the panicky look Constance had seen in her own reflection, when she'd stood and fought claustrophobia in front of the big window.

'You should go,' said Julia. 'If that's how you feel.' She turned to Constance. 'And you?'

'The same,' said Constance.

'I know,' said Julia. 'I have a very good theory of mind now. I can see right through you.'

Constance wanted to say something bitter, understood that it would be pointless, and decided not to. She reached out and shook Julia's hand.

'For what you were,' she said, 'even when you weren't.'

Julia clapped her shoulder. 'For what you'll be,' she said. 'Now go.'

'Goodbye, Mom,' said Constance. She and Andy went out, leaving the door open, and didn't look back.

'Any baggage?' asked the Long Tube guardian droid. It lived in a Faraday cage and had a manual-triggered Norton hardwired to its box. It wasn't going anywhere.

'Only this,' said Constance. She held up a flat metal rectangle the size of a business card.

'Contents?'

'Works of art.'

She and Andy had travelled half a light-year at half the speed of light. In the intervals of free flight – in the shuttle between the Inner Station and the Short Tube, and in the needle ship hurtling from the far end of the Inner Station No. 4 Short Tube to the deceleration port of the Long Station No. 1 Short Tube – they had scanned and sampled whatever they could detect of the huge and ever-increasing outpouring of information from the habitat haze. No longer green and gold, it now displayed an ever-changing rainbow flicker, reflecting and refracting the requirements of a population now far larger, and far from human. Some of what they had stored was scientific theory and technological invention, but by far the most valuable and comprehensible of it was art: music, pictures and designs produced by posthumans with a theory of mind so sophisticated that affecting human emotions more deeply than the greatest artists and composers of human history had ever done was its merest starting point, as elementary as drawing a line or playing a note. Constance knew that she now held in her hand enough stimulation and inspiration to trigger a renaissance wherever she went.

'Pass.'

Naked and hairless, carrying nothing but the metal card, Andy and Constance walked through the gate into the Long Tube needle ship. As they stepped over the lip of the airlock they both shivered. It was cold in the needle ship, and it was going to get a lot colder. Freezing to hibernate was the only way to live through the months of ten-gravity acceleration required to reach relativistic velocities; and the months of ten-gravity deceleration at the other end.

Travelling the Long Tube was like going down the steepest waterchute in the world. All she ever remembered of it was going

'Aaaahhhh!!!' for a very long time. The old hands called it the near-light scream.

Constance and Andy screamed to Barnard's Star. They screamed to Epsilon Eridani; to Tau Ceti; to Ross 248; to 61 Cygni. They kept going. The little metal memory device paid their way, in fares of priceless art and breakthrough discovery.

Eventually they emerged from the last of the Long Tubes. They had reached the surface of the expanding sphere of human civilization, from the inside. From here on out it was starships. The system was too poor as yet to build starships. It didn't even have many habitats. It had one habitable terrestrial: an Earthlike planet, if you could call a surface gravity of 1.5 and an ecosystem of pond scum Earthlike. People lived on it, in the open air.

Andy and Constance decided to give the place a try. They had to bulk up their bones and muscles, tweak every antibody in their immune systems, and cultivate new bacteria and enzymes in their guts. Doing all this kept them occupied in the long months of travel inward from the cometary cloud. It felt just like being seriously ill.

In this hemisphere, at this latitude, at this time of night, all the stars visible were without a habitat haze. They looked raw. They burned naked in different colours in the unbroken black dome of the sky.

Constance and Andy walked on slippery pebbles along the shore of a dark sea in which nothing lived but strands of algae and single-celled animals. On the shoreward side was a straggly windbreak of grass and shrubs, genetically modified from the native life, the greenish stuff that slimed the pebbles. A kilometre or two behind them lay the low buildings and dim lights of the settlement.

'All this living on rocks,' said Constance, 'sucks.'

'What's wrong with it?'

'Feeling heavy all the time. Weather that falls out of the sky instead of from ducts and sprinklers. Babies crying. Kids yelling. Dumb animals blundering about. Wavelengths from the sun I can't even tan against. I swear my skin's trying to turn blue. No roof over your head except when you're indoors. Meteors burning up in the air right above you.' She glanced balefully at the breakers. 'Oh, and repetitive meaningless noise.'

'I think,' said a voice in her earbead, 'that he's heard enough grumbles from you.'

Constance froze. Andy went on crunching forward along the stony beach.

'How did you get here?' Constance whispered.

'My partials remade me and transmitted me to you before you left the Solar system. Piggybacking the art codes. I really am Julia, just as I was before recent unfortunate events.'

'What do you want?'

'I have my genome,' said Julia. 'I want to download.'

'And then what?'

Constance could almost hear the shrug. 'To be a better mother?'

'Hah!'

'I also have some business ideas...'

'Mom,' said Constance, 'you can just forget it.'

She switched off the earbead. She would have to think about it.

She ran forward, in the awkward jarring way of someone carrying a half-grown child on their back.

'Sorry about the grumbles,' she said to Andy.

'Oh, that's all right,' he said. 'I feel the same sometimes. I think all that, and then I remember what makes up for it all.'

'What's that?' Constance smiled.

Andy looked up at her face, and she thought she knew what he was about to say, and then he looked farther up.

'The sky,' he said. 'The sky.'

Wilson at Woking

The Greek chick in the leathers had roared up on a Harley, her pretty blonde pal on the pillion carrying a bow and arrows. The girls were both minor royalty, and the buxom brunette had some military rank – honorary, of course, and not much excuse for being there, but I suppose HMG has to keep the colonels happy. The Greek and Portuguese military attachés were off on the far left, looking at the burning town through binoculars. Jerzy Kornel, from the Czechoslovak Embassy, was the only foreigner there I recognised. I waved and headed towards him.

Wilson stood in the centre of the trench, on a short stepladder that enabled him to peer over the top of the sandbags. Instantly recognisable with his trademark Gannex coat and Dunhill pipe, he talked to the Chief of Staff, Lord Montgomery, in a low voice just loud enough to carry to the microphones of the BBC and ITV crews who crouched a few yards away. I caught a snatch of it as I scurried past, head down:

'Alamein,' he was saying, flattering the old poser, who (typically) was standing one step higher on his own stepladder, 'I frankly don't see anything the RAF can't handle.'

'But, Prime Minister, my chaps are ready at a moment's notice to...'

Close by, a likewise earnest and public exchange was going on between a Brigadier and a white-haired scientist, eccentric in Carnaby Street Edwardian rig. I overheard some remark from the latter about sticky-tape across windows as a precaution against nuclear blast.

It was all for the benefit of the masses glued to the box.

Morale boosting, very much needed after the images of the refugee columns streaming towards London, and the heat-rays flickering from the gigantic, half-buried cylinders on Horsell Common. So far, the word 'Martians' hadn't passed any official lips, but that hadn't stopped speculation, some of it even wilder.

I picked my way past the tangled cables of the TV OBUs. Jerzy wore a black velvet smoking-jacket over the olive-green shirt and trousers of a Czechoslovak People's Army uniform. He held out a cigarette pack and tapped.

'Light up an Embassy.' Grinning, he flicked his Ronson for me then gave me what was for him a serious look. His voice was barely audible above the thud of the Beeb's generator, and the distant roar of the Vulcans circling below the horizon.

'Do you think it's the Russians?'

'Harold was on the red phone first thing,' I said, as if I'd been at his elbow rather than having heard the rumour third-hand. 'He's positive it's not. Word from the top. Straight from the Kremlin's onion domes, old boy.'

'He trusts Brezhnev,' said Jerzy, more sourly than seemed appropriate.

'Well, naturally,' I said. 'These two go all the way back to Helm's Deep.'

I didn't need to allude to the other battles of the Second World War in which Wilson, Brezhnev, and Kennedy – the Big Three, as my father's generation called them – had forged their unbreakable alliance, shoulder to shoulder against the Weimar Germans' cyborg hordes and genetically engineered slave races.

'They've had their differences since.'

I laughed. 'The PM likes to say that when you've faced down the National Union of Boilermakers...'

Jerzy shrugged one shoulder. 'Spare me. So who is it?'

A heat-ray scorched the air overhead, setting alight a gorse-bush half a mile behind us.

'That,' I said, 'is what you might call the burning question.'

My presence at what later came to be called the Battle of Woking was pure chance, though no more so than the presence of most of those who'd turned up for what was as much a media circus as a national emergency. How a research assistant for the Fabian Society found himself working in 10 Downing Street is not worth recounting here – such sudden preferments were part and parcel of the Wilson style of government, aiming to circumvent the senior civil servants, conservative to a man. So it was that I found myself in the cramped back seat of a black Morris Minor at the tail end of the cavalcade of official cars that trundled out of Central London and sped down the M3 and M25 that fine May morning.

The three cylinders had arrived the night before, and the Fighting Machines had begun to lay waste to Woking almost as soon as the first lid had slowly unscrewed and toppled to the grass. The Astronomer Royal, Sir Patrick Moore, had rushed to the midnight emergency meeting of Wilson's notorious 'kitchen Cabinet' with what he claimed were photographs from a few weeks earlier of mysterious flashes on the planet Mars. They'd been wired from the Royal Observatory near Edinburgh, in North Britain. To the untrained eye the plates showed little more than a cracked sphere, with notable imperfections in resolution, but Sir Patrick assured us that he'd identified the source of the flashes as a major confluence of canals, and probable population centre, located as it was in the midst of a particularly lush area of Martian vegetation.

'This lush vegetation of yours,' said Harold, stabbing at the blurry, over-enlarged photo with the stem of his pipe, 'seems to have vanished from the latest picture.'

'Precisely!' cried Sir Patrick, eyebrows twitching like the wings of a demented hen. 'The fields have been stripped bare to supply the expedition! This is the last throw of a dying race, gentlemen! We are in serious danger!'

'Well then,' Harold growled, 'it's about bloody time we went out and had a look.'

It had taken the redoubtable Marcia Falkender to talk him into at least waiting until the troops had surrounded the area. Which, over the remaining hours of the night, the Surrey Regiment – known since the Peninsular War as Sharpe's Rifles – had very competently done. Though not without cost; a Fighting Machine and a Chieftain tank were a terrifyingly even match. A direct hit from one could destroy the other. After a few such exchanges, each side had pulled back – the Fighting Machines to the cylinders, the troops and tanks to hastily constructed trenches and berms. Hence the current stand-off.

It couldn't last. Aerial photography had revealed that some process of manufacture – of more Fighting Machines, presumably – was going on inside the cylinders, but the heat rays had shot down too many brave pilots for even the RAF to dare to attempt to discern anything further. Beyond the heat-rays' reach, the Vulcans circled, awaiting the dreadful order to expend their hydrogen bombs – after, I could only hope, everyone had fled the area, and all the windows of London had been secured with sticky tape.

Jerzy stubbed out his cigarette on the side of the trench.

'No,' he said. 'The burning question isn't who they are. The burning question is what they have against gorse bushes.'

I laughed.

'I'm serious,' he said. 'Their first targets – after the foolish gawpers – were the trees on the Common, and in the town's gardens and parks. They'll aim the heat-rays at a tank or plane in the open, but not at tanks behind sand-bags. Now they're burning the bushes. Why?'

'To create a conflagration, obviously, and the cover of smoke.' I coughed, not from the gasper. 'A tactic they're succeeding in.'

'They could aim at cars or houses, which are far more inflammable. Instead, they attack vegetation.'

Vegetation... something about that nagged at my mind.

'They stripped vegetation from around their launch sites –' I began, then belatedly shut up.

"They'?' Jerzy quirked an eyebrow. 'Ah, so you do know who they are!'

'It's speculative,' I said.

'So? Tell me!'

I told him of Moore's claims. To my surprise, he didn't scoff. Instead, he leaned forward and spoke quietly.

'This all makes sense now,' he murmured. 'The Russians landed a space probe on Mars last month.'

I yelped. 'My God, man! Why don't we know of this?'

'They intended to keep it quiet until all the results were in, then announce it with much fanfare at the Party congress in October.' He shrugged. 'You know the Russians. Everything's for propaganda advantage.'

'How do *you* know about it?' I asked.

Jerzy tapped the side of his nose. 'Here is a Czech riddle: are the Russians our friends, or our brothers?'

I shook my head.

'Our brothers! You *choose* your friends.'

I laughed politely. 'But what's the connection between the Russian probe and – this?'

'The Russian probe,' said Jerzy, 'was atomic-powered. Who knows what damage it may have done? This' – he waved his arm around at the scene – 'is more than a return visit. It's retaliation.'

A sudden commotion interrupted us – yells, screams, a distant thud of artillery. Whirling around, and recklessly stretching to see over the lip of the trench, I saw Fighting Machines swarm from the cylinders like newly hatched flies from carrion. Their previous striding motion had been replaced by a remarkable, rapid bobbing-and-weaving: they simply *dodged* the tanks' shells. I ducked hard and fast as the heat-ray barrage intensified overhead into a grid of fire.

Everyone in the trench had likewise crouched, or thrown themselves flat in the mud. We all cowered, even Lord Montgomery. All – except Wilson. He stood one step higher on the ladder, pipe in one hand and a bulky walkie-talkie clutched in the other.

'Now, Tony!' I heard him shout. 'Now!'

From all around us, a sound arose that overwhelmed the noises of the distant jets, the shelling, the generator, the screams. It was the most fearsome racket I'd ever heard in my life. I looked up, just in time to be blasted head over heels by a ferocious down-draught from something enormous that passed about six feet above the top of the trench.

I picked myself up, and – inspired perhaps by Wilson's still unflinching demeanour – lunged to the front of the trench and hauled myself up to peer over. Dozens of grey-painted, armour-plated hovercraft, each about half the size of a house, were hurtling from all directions around the Common. They moved so fast that they were in among the Fighting Machines in seconds. Their prows sliced at the tripods' legs, knocking them down like ninepins.

But as I watched, I saw Fighting Machines that had been knocked down struggle to their feet. Their heat-rays still slashed the sky. Whenever a ray hit one of the hovercraft, it left a visible scorch from which smoke drifted. I could just make out the red-hot craters left in the hulls of these land ironclads. No ray had penetrated yet, but it could be only a matter of moments before the Martians improved their aim and learned to repeat their shots.

Then I saw an astonishing thing. I don't think anyone else did:

only Wilson was cool enough, and I unhinged enough, to be looking. A few tens of yards away, the leather-clad Greek girl hoisted her slender friend – foot in cupped hands – right on to the edge of the trench. There the blonde stood, clad only in her flimsy minidress, and shot off in rapid succession a score or two of arrows from the quiver on her shoulder.

Each arrow flew unerringly to some joint or other in a Fighting Machine. And one by one, the terrible tripods toppled, not to rise again. The whole thing was over in about a minute. A silence fell, broken only by a mournful hooting from the felled machines, and a moment later by the roar of a departing motorcycle.

The day afterwards, it turned out that Brezhnev had taken the opportunity of the distraction to move Russian armoured divisions into Prague. Jerzy was beside himself. I took him to Number 10, in breach of all protocol.

Wilson picked up the red phone.

'Leonid,' he snarled, '*get your tanks off my lawn!*'

And, incredibly, Brezhnev agreed.

There's little further to add. Except this: Wilson always attributed the victory to himself and to Tony Benn's armoured atomic hovercraft, which had melted the Martian invaders in the white heat of the technological revolution. He knew as well as I did that this wasn't true. But that's how it went into the history books – and we all know about them.

'The history books will be kind to me,' Wilson used to chuckle. 'I know, because I'll write them.'

And, of course, he did.

~

Note: this story is dedicated to that small, happy percentage of my compatriots who (according to a recent survey) believe that the Prime Minister of Great Britain during the Second World War was Harold Wilson; that the Battle of Helm's Deep, the War of the Worlds, Xena, and Richard Sharpe were real historical events and persons; and that the Battle of the Bulge, William Wallace, Adolf Hitler, and the Cold War were not.

Sidewinders

1. The Trafalgar Gate

I bought a kilo of oranges in Soho – Covent Garden would have none at this time of year – and walked down Whitcomb Street and around the corner on Pall Mall to the Square. The Gate faced me, a concrete henge straddling the entrance to Duncannon Street. There wasn't much of a queue, just a line four abreast filling the pavement along the front of the National Gallery and St Martin's in the Fields. I passed the two hours it took me to get to the front reading the latest Amis *fils* in paperback. I turned the last page and chucked the Penguin to a hurrying, threadbare art student seconds before I'd have had to relinquish the book to the security bin.

'Papers, please.'

I resisted the temptation to monkey the guard's cockney. String bag slung on the thumb, rope of my duffel bag clutched in the fingers of one hand, I passed the documents over with the other, for a frowning moment of scrutiny. Then the guard waved me on to the Customs table. Wanded, searched, duffel bag contents spread out and thrust back in any old how. Passport scanned and stamped. One orange taken 'for random inspection'. I've paid worse tolls. As long as the stack of Marie Therese thalers and the small change in my boot-heels made it through, I was good to go anywhere.

I walked under the arch and into Scotland.

They don't like you to call it Scotland, of course. Officially, East London is the capital of the GBR (which – the tired joke notwithstanding – doesn't actually stand for 'Gordon Brown's Republic' but is the full name of the state, derived from the standard ISO abbreviation for 'Great Britain' and accepted as its legal designation at the exhausted end of the 1978 UN Security Council session that imposed the settlement, ending the bloody civil war that followed the Colonels' Coup of '73). But it's mostly Scottish accents you hear on the streets, along with Asian and African and Islingtonian – the few thousand white working-class Londoners who stayed in the East are in high demand as faces and voices for the regime: actors, diplomats, border guards. North Britain (another name they don't like) speaks to the world in a cockney accent.

I walked up Duncannon Street, avoiding eye contact with anyone in a plastic fake-leather jacket. The bank is still called the Royal Bank and the currency is still called the pound. Come to think of it, the Party is still called Labour. Zig-zagging the Strand and Kingsway, I was a hundred metres from Holborn when I noticed I was being followed. Usual stuff – corner of the eye, shop-window reflection, tail still there after I'd dashed across the four lanes (GBR traffic's mercifully two-stroke, and sparse) and walked on. Worse, when I checked again in a parked wing-mirror the guy vanished in plain sight. (In *my* plain sight, that is. No one else noticed.)

Another sidewinder, then. One who knew I was on to him. Shit. Jack Straw's boys (and girls) I could dodge with my eyes shut. This was different.

There's a procedure for everything. For this situation, SOP is to take a long step sideways – chances are, the sidewinder who's spotted you spotting him has just hopped into an adjacent probability (like, one where you took a different route) and is sprinting ahead to hop back further up the road (following *his* SOP, natch). But he'd know that, so if he knew I was a sidewinder... but I had no evidence of that, yet. Either way, the trick was to take a bigger or a smaller jump than he'd expect, but one that would still keep me on track to catch an Edinburgh train at King's Cross.

I turned sharp left onto High Holborn and walked briskly towards the border. Long before I'd reached Princes Circus, I was the only person on the street. There isn't a wall between East and West London – they've learned that much – but planning blight, student hostels, and regular patrols fill the function almost as well. From a sidewinder's angle, though, the good thing about the band of run-down property east of Charing Cross Road is that it's a debatable land, a place where the probabilities are manifold, and therefore a prime locale for long sideways steps.

I clambered over concrete rubble, waded through fireweed, crunched broken panes, and stood still and did that thing in my head.

2. That thing in my head

You do it too.

Those times when you *know* you left the front-door keys on the kitchen table, not beside the phone, and there's no one else around who *could* have moved them? Big secret: it wasn't the little people messing with your head. That street entrance or shop front you've never noticed before, though you must have driven past it a hundred times? Shock revelation: you're not living *The Truman Show*, and nobody's shifting the scenery.

You're shifting, *in* the scenery: sideslipping between entire universes whose only difference may be where you left the keys last night, or how a town plan turned out thirty years ago, or a planning permission last month, or...

You're doing it all the time, unconsciously. Sidewinders do it consciously. Don't ask me how, or how many of us there are. You don't want to know. Most of us, by a sort of natural selection, end up in the probability where they're happy, or at least content. A small minority are intrinsically malcontent, or seduced by the possibilities, or both.

Some of that minority get recruited. You don't want to know about that, either. Let's just say there are two sides. Well, there are an infinity of sides, but they collapse, on inspection, to two: the Improvers, and the Conservers.

The Improvers want to put 'wrong' histories 'back on track'; the Conservers want all possible histories to unfold unhindered. This conflict has, I'm told, been going on for some time. I suspect it's waged from great shining bastions of widely separated probability where civilization is vastly more advanced than it is anywhere we can reach, each of them perhaps far outside the human branch of history altogether. The best-laid plans of Miocene men, or of the wily descendants of dinosaurs on an Earth the asteroid missed...

That's the sort of question we sidewinders argue amongst ourselves. For you, for now – all you need to know is, I'm an Improver.

And right now I was on the run from a Conserver.

3. Tairlidhe is my darlin', the young chevalier

I stepped out of the bank doorway I found myself in, nodded to the footman, and caught a tram. Tall buildings, fat with sandstone and gross with gilt, filled the view from the top-deck window. The streets buzzed with electric velocipedes and reeked with ethanol-fuelled cars. The pavements were more crowded than those of the world I'd come from, and the crowds whiter. Here and there a Mahometan, a Hindoo or a Jew walked, distinct in their costume and dignity. Blacks and Chinese were more common and less noticeable, porters and street-merchants for the most part. Slavery was abolished in 1836, after the Virginia Insurrection made it too expensive; the Opium Wars were never fought.

Discreetly, I unscrewed a boot-heel and thumb-nailed out a 1997 shilling with the head of Charles X. The conductor grumbled, but gave me a fistful of nickel in change that weighed down my jacket pocket as I jumped off. King's Cross is in the same place, with the same name – it's one of those sites that's a converse to the debatable lands: a place implacable, straddling probabilities like railway lines. The statue in the front is of Luipoldt II.

I plunged to the ticket office through the fetid cloud of pomade and pipe-smoke and bought a single to Edinburgh. Display-boards clattered with flip-plates of digits and destinations. An express at 12 of the clock, platform 3. I bought a newspaper and a packed lunch, and took my seat. The train – French-fangled, electric – glided out as all the church-bells of London pealed noon, flashed through the villages north of London – Camden, Islington, Newington – at an accelerating clip that reached a hundred and fifty miles an hour as we passed Barnet. Too fast to read the sign, but I knew the town. There's always, for me, a *frisson* at Barnet – it's where the last battle of the Second Restoration was fought, when the Bonny Prince and his men routed the Hornsey militia and found London defenceless before them.

The endless fields of England rolled by, the spring ploughing well under way, sometimes with one man behind a horse, sometimes with a great modern contraption from the Massey manufactories, drawn by a phalanx of Clydesdales. I leaned on the table, munched bread and cheese and sipped stout, and worried idly about my soft spot for this probability. How does one weigh the absence of total war and totalitarian revolution, against the continuance of Caliph and Romanoff and Manchu, and Voltaire at Ferney broken on the wheel?

I was in the non-smoking carriage, with the ladies, which didn't bother me at all. My clothes, while unfashionable, raised no more than a momentary eyebrow. A bum-freezer here is a pea-jacket there, and Levi makes denim jeans across a surprising range of probabilities.

Across the table – not Pullman, but the idea is obvious enough – sat a young lady, bowed over a thick book. Black brows knitted under her bonnet, lips moving as she read, her thin face pallid, her gown frayed at the cuffs. She glanced up as I turned a rustling page of *The Times*, and I smiled politely and looked back at the science page. Antarctic continent found – Spanish claim disputed. The young woman sighed. I looked up again.

'A heroine in jeopardy, milady?' I asked.

She shot me an indignant glance.

'I am not reading a *novel*,' she said. 'I study zoology.'

'Ah,' I said. 'Your pardon. An admirable pursuit.'

'But it is so hard!' she cried. 'All those lists!'

'The Latin names,' I murmured, nodding sagely, 'of the great Linnaeus? They can indeed be a trial – '

She shook her head. 'It is not that. So many disconnected facts to commit to memory!' Then she frowned. 'I cannot place your accent, sir.'

'New Scotland,' I said, with a self-deprecating smile. 'Hence the barbaric twang.'

She took this bold-faced lie without demur. I told another.

'My name,' I said, 'is Steve Jones.'

'And mine,' she said, 'is Mary Ann Dykes.'

'At your service, miss.'

'Thank you. Delighted to make your acquaintance.'

I gave my occupation, disingenuously, as commercial traveller in oranges. She gave hers as confidential servant.

'And why, if I may make so bold, are you studying zoology?'

'I am an orphan, sir,' she said. 'I say this not to elicit sympathy, but to explain. I go to seek a post as a governess, in the Scottish capital. The mistress of the house has ambitions for her sons to be physicians, and I have been told that comparative anatomy is – but no!' She smiled suddenly. 'That is true, but merely my excuse. The subject intrigues me.'

'As I said, an admirable pursuit.'

'But most taxing. Before my father passed away, he taught me the rudiments of mathematics, and of Newton. Would that zoology had its Newton!'

'I know little of that science,' I mused aloud, 'but I have sometimes thought that, just as our poor will multiply to the limits of their wages, or of the poor-rates, the entire brute creation must perforce indulge in an even more wanton and thoughtless reproduction of their kind...'

Mary Ann didn't blush. This history had no Victoria. She frowned.

'Yes?' she said. 'Your drift, sir?'

'Yet as we see,' I went on, 'the world is not over-run with' – I glanced out of the window – 'rabbits, let us say, or nettles. All that are born do not survive, and those who do must, on average, have some perhaps slight advantage which – so to speak – *selects* them for survival over their less fit brethren. If we dare to imagine this process repeated, generation after generation, over many ages and revolutions of the Earth... but I fear I am rushing too far, in too speculative a direction.'

'No!' she said. She clutched my wrist, then withdrew her too-hasty hand. This time, she did blush. 'Please, do go on.'

I did. By the time we reached the southern shore of the Firth of Forth, her textbook was covered with delighted scribbles linking facts at last, and her face with astonished smiles and happy frowns at the results.

I was about to part with her, at the station – which is called simply Edinburgh Central, Walter Scott in this world having remained an advocate at the Bar – smug in my Improving zeal, when she caught my elbow.

'Mr Jones,' she said, 'may I presume upon our acquaintance to ask you to escort me to my destination? It is in the West Port, and –' She looked away.

'And the Grassmarket is notorious for footpads, and you cannot afford a cab? Don't worry, Miss Dykes. I can't afford one either. Let us walk together.'

I carried her luggage. It was pathetically light.

'Mr Jones,' she inquired anxiously as we emerged from the rear of the station on to Market Street and caught our first stagnant whiff of the Nor Loch, 'I see you carry no weapon.'

'I need none,' I assured her. 'I am an adept in the martial arts of the East.'

She laughed. 'Ancient arts are no match for a good pistol, sir, but I still trust in your protection.'

Across the Royal Mile, down St Mary's Street into the Cowgate, then along beneath the North Bridge and Charles IV Bridge toward the Grassmarket. High, dank walls like cliff-faces dripped. Opium dens wafted their dark allure. Gypsy fiddles enlivened the air around hostelries. Homeward cars and velocipedes splashed through the noxious puddles. After the Cowgate, the Grassmarket was respectability itself, even with its tinker stalls, beggar families, skulking footpads, stilt-walking clowns, and carousing students of medicine, divinity and law. The flag of the Three Kingdoms, aflutter in the evening breeze, could be glimpsed over the Castle which, like its Rock, straddles history sturdy and aloof with only its flags changing, above the Grassmarket's seething pool of probabilities.

Out of that seething pool stepped my pursuer. Two metres in front of us, and no one in between. If I hadn't recognised his face, the levelled thing in his hand would have identified him surely enough. In this world, it might have seemed no more than a glittering toy, but Mary Ann divined its sinister import in an instant. Or perhaps she just reacted to my start. She clutched my upper arm with both hands. From the point of view of one about to draw on the martial arts of the East, this was not a welcome move, however pleasing it might have been under other circumstances.

After a split second of bafflement, I realised that my pursuer must have stayed in the GBR, guessed – or been leaked – my destination – and blithely taken the faster train of that more advanced world, then sidestepped to this world of Tairlidhe's victory to await me. How he'd found out that this was the world to which I'd fled to evade him, I didn't care to guess. Infiltration and defection are permanent possibilities, across all probabilities.

I had no choice. I sidestepped, back to the GBR. I may have hoped my pursuer wouldn't expect that, but in all honesty it was a reflex.

I had never before sidestepped with someone holding on to me. I was almost as surprised as Mary Ann to find us still together, in a different Grassmarket.

'What is this?' she cried, gazing around bewildered at the suddenly airier, cleaner, brighter and even noisier space of the plaza. She let go off me, and took a swift pace or two back and looked at me with suspicion and dread. 'What arts of the East have you used, Mr Jones? Sorcery? Illusion?'

'Not these, I fear,' I said. 'This is real. It is a different reality than that to which you are accustomed – one in which history took a different turn, centuries ago.'

She seemed to grasp the concept at once.

'Are there many such?'

'An infinite number,' I told her.

'But how marvellous! And yet how obvious, that the Creator's infinity should be reflected in His creations!'

'That's one way of looking at it,' I allowed.

Mary Ann looked around again, more calmly now, though I could see her quivering.

'I see this is a history in which the Covenanters' memory is honoured,' she said. She pointed to one of a trio of statues. 'I recognise that visage, of Richard Cameron. But who are the others?'

'They will mean nothing to you,' I said.

'I want to see them, all the same.'

She was intrigued by the pedestrian crossing, and impressed by the vehicles, tinny and two-stroke though they were. I nudged her to stop her staring at women with bare heads and short skirts. We stopped beneath the statues.

The stern man in the homburg, with upraised, didactic, forefinger:

'"John Maclean",' she read from the plinth. 'A preacher, was he?'

'In a manner of speaking,' I said. 'And in his manner of public speech, by all accounts.'

The man in the short coat, with glasses and pipe – and, Scotland being Scotland in all manifestations, with a traffic cone on his head:

'And "Harold Wilson, martyr of British democracy"?' She

recoiled almost, frowning. 'A *democrat?* A radical?'

'Not precisely,' I said, looking around distractedly. 'It would take too long to explain. That man who confronted us – he may catch up at any moment. I must go.'

'What about me, Mr Jones?' Mary Ann said.

'I'm sorry,' I said, still looking about. 'I can't take you with me. It's far too dangerous. You'll be safe here for now.' My gaze alighted on a tall concrete building, from which hung a banner with a jowly, frowning, face and the letters 'GB'. I pointed.

'Remove your bonnet,' I said. 'It's not customary here. Your dress will pass. Go to that building, ask for the Women's Institute, and say that you have just arrived from London, penniless. Say nothing of where you really come from, lest you be consigned to a lunatic asylum. You will be made welcome, and given employment. Learn what you can in this world, and as soon as possible I'll take you back to yours.'

'But –'

Out of the corner of my eye, I saw my pursuer emerge from the pub called The Last Drop, and peer around.

'Goodbye, Miss Dykes,' I said.

I handed her the oranges – they were for here, after all, where they were scarce – and sidestepped as far as I'd ever dared in a single jump.

4. Storm Constantinople!

And fell briefly into a world of Latin buzz and blazing neon, of fairy lights suspended on nothing above a grassy park, on which robe-clad dark-skinned people strolled beneath a Rock with no Castle, and with an evening sky alight with the artificial constellations of celestial cities in orbit overhead. I sprinted across the sward, towards where the King's Stables Road wouldn't be. I'd never been in this probability, but I recognised it by report: this is the one where Spartacus won, slavery fell, capitalism rose, and the Romans reached the Moon in about 500 (Not) A.D. and Alpha Centauri a century or two later...

I leaped a stream that in most other worlds had long since been a sewer, sidestepped in mid-air, in a familiar but much less hopeful direction, and came down with a skid and a thud on dust and ash. I stumbled, flailing, and trod on a circle of glowing embers which I as quickly jumped out of, scattering more ash.

'Oi!' someone shouted. It must have been his fire.

'Sorry!' over my shoulder. Then I ran without looking back. Around me the early evening was lit only by scattered small fires, some of them behind the window-spaces of what buildings remained standing. Grass and weeds poked through the crazed tarmac under my feet. A few metres in front of me, a random leaf of grass or scrap of paper caught fire. I threw myself forward, hitting the ground with a pain I wouldn't feel for minutes. I side-stepped into an adjacent probability, as one might roll on the ground, got up and ran on.

The Improver base in this Edinburgh lies beneath where a multi-storey park had been, close to the unaltered Castle Rock. I reached the door – saw a red bead on the wall – flinched aside – keyed the code in the lock – dived through.

I stood up in low fluorescent lighting, pale corridors. I suspected my pursuer would be after me. I rang the alarm. Two guards were ready for him when he slipped into our space from a probability where the car park's floors hadn't pancaked in the blast from Rosyth. His capture took only a moment: a hiss of gas, a thrown net, the laser pistol knocked from his fingers.

The guards tied him in the net to a chair. I tried to interrogate him, before the effects of the gas wore off and he gathered his wits enough to sidestep.

'Why are you after me?'

His head jerked, his eyes rolled, his tongue lolled. 'Isn't it obvious? You were on a mission to undermine the GBR!'

'What's that to you?' I said. 'To Conservers, that regime must be an abomination anyway – radical, revolutionary even – isn't that everything you're against?'

'No, no.' He struggled to focus his eyes and control his drool. 'It's a rare marvel. A socialist state that works, that has survived the fall of Communism, because of the computerised planning developed at Strathclyde from the ideas of Kantorovich and Neurath. You have no idea, do you, where that might lead? Nor do we, but we want to find out.'

'Well,' I said, 'sorry about that, old boy, very interesting no doubt, but I'm fucked if my relatives will suffer in this Caledonian Cuba a second longer than they have to.'

He inhaled snot. 'Fuck you.'

I could see I wouldn't get much more out of him, so I whiled the minutes before he recovered enough to slip away by taunting him with what I'd done on the train. He looked at me with horror and loathing.

'You introduced *Darwin* to that world?'

'Who?' I said. 'Wallace's theory of natural selection – that's what I outlined.'

He thrashed in the net. 'Whoever. You know what you may have done, if that young woman should be the one who convinces that world that evolution happened? Some day, perhaps many years hence, in some backwater of an Eastern empire, a young man – an Orthodox seminarian in Georgia, perhaps – will read her work, lose his faith, and go on to lead a bloody revolution –'

'– which will happen anyway, in one or other of these shit-holes,' I said. 'We're working on that problem.'

'I wish you luck,' he said drily. He was coming to, now, almost ready to vanish before our eyes.

'And what about this world?' I demanded. 'This post-atomic horror? Would you have us leave it too?'

'Yes,' he said. 'To see what comes of it. Let it be.'

And he went. The net slumped to the chair. I looked at the guards, shrugged.

'*C'est la vie*,' one of them said. 'Come on, you need a coffee. And some bandages.'

I followed them to the first aid station, then to the canteen. As I sipped hot black coffee, I found myself gazing idly at the room's walls, which were papered with old newspaper and magazine pages, saved from ruins. A particularly striking front page of the *Daily Mirror*, from May 1968, showed four long-haired young people in white T-shirts with a big black cross, which in a colour picture would have been red. The caption identified the youths as Andreas Baader, Ulrike Meinhof, Bernadette Devlin, and Danny Cohn-Bendit. They stood on a platform in front of a huge crowd, the wind blowing in their hair, AK-47s in their uplifted hands, and behind them the skyline of Istanbul. The city in whose streets they would, a few hours later, fall to a hail of machine-gun bullets – along with a shocking proportion of the youthful crowd.

What good could come, I thought, of probability as crazy as this? One in which Pope Paul VI had responded to the Israeli victory in the Six-Day War of 1967 by claiming Palestine again for the Church, and urged the youth of Europe on a Crusade to win it back? A crusade that had ended with an assault on Istanbul, a city too stubborn to let the human tide through? And where the massacre had sparked an international incident that had escalated to an all-out thermonuclear exchange?

While worlds like that – and worse – exist, I remain an Improver.

I caught up with Mary Ann Dykes a few weeks later, on another of my jaunts to the Republic. I'd made my dead-letter drops for the dissidents, I had a spare few hours, and I sought her out. I found her working in a women's refugee centre, giving, as she put it, something back for the help she'd been given. Her hair was trimmed, her skirt short, her cheeks pink, her habits unladylike. I spoke to her outside, as she took a cigarette break on the street. She'd applied for a place at Glasgow, to study zoology.

'I can take you back,' I told her. 'Back to your own world, where the knowledge you've picked up can make you famous, and rich.'

She sucked hard on her cigarette and looked at me as if I were crazy. She waved a hand at the street, all ruts and litter and Party posters flapping in the breeze and GB's face and Straw's surveillance cameras everywhere.

'Why?' she demanded. 'I like it here.'

There's pleasing some people, that's the trouble.

The Surface of Last Scattering

I have no memories of my father. He left our lives when I was three and a half years old. My earliest recollection – my mother's red coat, me on a swing – is from about six months later. Nothing remarkable in that: childhood amnesia is almost universal. All I have of him from my earliest years is a photograph. And that is remarkable.

I walk into Glasgow Queen Street Station with a good half hour to spare, buy a coffee, and settle on a steel bench as far back from the ticket barriers as possible. This isn't very far. I have a clear view of the platform where the train will come in from Carstairs, and where in twenty minutes my father will step off and come through, looking for me. I have no idea what he looks like, and he – as far as I know – has none of me. It's our phones that will, discreetly, recognise each other. The Prison Service has helpfully set that up, and has been likewise helpful in releasing him an unpublicised couple of months before the end of his sentence. Even their refusal to give me a picture of him has been well-intentioned – they don't want the smallest possibility of a hack or a leak. They want to give him a chance. His face was once the best-known in the world. In a way, that works in his favour. Everyone knows his appearance at the time of his trial. Nobody has seen a picture of him since. Even the screws and lags have been prevailed upon not to give anyone as much as a sketch. He'll have changed a lot in fifteen years (minus sixty-one days). Of course, anyone can run an app to predict his current appearance. But still, he has a chance of at least some breathing space, of days or weeks to find his feet before he's recognised and the media siege begins.

Fifteen years. My God! For most of these years, I didn't even know about him. I didn't know that the guy my mother was married to, and who'd been around almost as long as I can remember, wasn't my father. Not that I have any complaints about Joe, he's been a good parent and everything; I love the guy I suppose, but he's not my father. I don't blame him or my mother for not telling me until I was fourteen and old enough to take the truth.

If indeed I had been old enough. Looking back with all the maturity of my eighteen years, adulthood practically, I wonder if I haven't been obsessed.

I pop the top of the plastic cup and look for a place to dispose of the wet lid. No bins within reach, as usual, and I don't want to lose my seat. I place the lid furtively between my feet, and sit back a little to sniff and sip the hot java. The bench's back seems (and, now I come to think of it, may quite rationally have been) designed to be uncomfortable, angled so you can't lean against it without its edge pressing painfully against your spine. I sit up straight. My gaze drifts upward to the station's domed roof. It was famous once. Twenty-odd years ago, it was among the first pieces of architecture to use a light-bending metamaterial to create public art. The first such dome – in Bilbao, I think – showed the stars and planets and satellites above, night and day, far more sharply and abundantly than you could actually see them from the city streets even on a clear night. So did the second, the more famous one at Shenzhen. The starry sky was in danger of becoming a cliché. The next big dome was of the radio sky, and that, in turn... Glasgow's city council went for something different.

That's why, above me, the domed roof shows a shifting, fuzzy pattern of false colour, mostly shades of grey, with a few glimmers of red and yellow here and there. It seems to hang in the air: you can't see the dome itself, just the image it forms.

It was a sensation, for a while. But now, I'm the only person looking up at it. No one else spares it a glance. No wonder. It's impressive as a concept, and if you know what it is: the part of the cosmic microwave background in the sky directly overhead. You're looking back in time as far as it's possible to look, almost to the point where the photons first escaped. And it's real, extracted by the subtle warp of the metamaterial from the radiation that filters through the atmosphere, somewhat distorted but the real deal: the afterglow of the Big Bang, the first light from fourteen point whatever billion years ago. But visually, it's just like a cloudy sky, with a little sunshine breaking through. Typical Glasgow summer weather, in other words. The dome might as well have been transparent.

I look again at the Arrivals board. Twelve minutes to go. I keep wondering if I'll recognise my father. I can't help myself – I reach into my inside jacket pocket and pull out the old photograph. The laminating plastic is a little scuffed, and the pigments have faded, but it's still clear enough. A young man with longish curly brown hair, a fuzzy beard, and glasses, looking into the face of a baby cradled in his arm. The man is smiling and the baby is looking straight back into his eyes.

'That's a cool device,' says an interested, amused female voice at my shoulder. I turn sharply. Coffee, fortunately no longer scalding, splashes on the back of my hand. The girl's about my age or maybe a year or two younger. Her face is not exactly pretty but lively, and carefully made-up, framed by short black hair.

She's wearing a sort of creamy-coloured shiny smock with frilly shoulders, over black long-sleeved top and leggings. She has tats on her wrists and piercings in her ear-lobes and a black nylon bag at her feet.

Now I know – from bitter experience of past missed opportunities – that when a lassie sits down beside you and says something out of the blue, she very probably fancies you. I also know, with a likewise bitter certainty, that this is going to be another missed opportunity.

'Uh, it's not a device,' I say, letting her see it, wishing I could hide it. 'It's a printed photo laminated in plastic. That's why it hasn't…'

'Oh!' she says. 'Like, on paper? Wow! I've never seen one. I really did think it was a phone or something.'

'It's just a photo,' I say, sounding surly even to myself. I make to slip it back in my inside pocket, but she catches hold of the edge.

'It's a sweet picture,' she says. 'And it's from before the Rot, so it must be – oh! That's you, isn't it?'

'Yes,' I admit. I ease the photo from her grip and put it away. She looks a bit hurt and puzzled. I say something to ease my embarrassment.

'So now you've seen my baby picture.'

Now she's the one who looks embarrassed. She looks away. I glance again at the display above the ticket barrier. (Funny how we still call them 'ticket' barriers.) The train is due in five minutes.

'I can see you're waiting for someone,' she says, getting up. 'Sorry to bother you.'

'No, wait…'

But she's off, towards the mall that semi-circles the station's perimeter. In a moment her back has vanished in the contra-flow of hurry. And I don't even know her name, let alone her number.

I sigh, drain the cup, crush it and drop it. I wonder if she's guessed that I'm waiting for someone from Carstairs. The place is no longer a secure mental hospital. It's just a long-stay, high-security prison, but it still has that sinister reputation. Anyone who's been in Carstairs is deemed to be a psychopath or worse. I take out my phone and flick through the document folders (another of those archaic, pre-Rot terms...) of background and evidence. My father has never replied to my emails with all these heavy attachments, and never shown any interest in using what I sent him to appeal. But surely, now that he's out...

Two minutes. I stand up and take a dozen strides forward, to where I can see along the platform but I'm not in the way of people going on. The train pulls in. Hundreds of people flood towards the exit gates. I feel very self-conscious as my eyes flick from one hurrying man to another. Some of them give me a curious look back, and I look away. Then, to my surprise, I recognise my father. He's lost the beard. Thin, crop-haired, balding, early forties. New suit, rolling case. He's not in a hurry; he's looking around, taking things in. His eyes don't meet mine. He saunters through the barrier with a wave of his plastic, steps out of the flow on the other side, and stands on the station concourse, a few metres away. He pats a pocket, takes out a phone, glances down and then at me. My own phone buzzes at the same moment.

A smile. I nod. We dodge through the still-emerging passengers, and converge. Handshakes, awkward one-arm-around-the-shoulders hug. He steps back and looks at me.

'Conal! How great to see you! Thanks for coming.'

'Good to see you, uh, father.'

I can't call him 'Dad'. I've called Joe that for too long.

'"Keith" is fine,' he says. He glances around.

'Hasn't changed much,' he says. 'Except... ah, the departure board displays.' He gazes up at these as if in wonder, nods, then turns back to me.

'Coffee, somewhere nearby, posh, bit of privacy?'

I gesture towards the semi-circular mall.

'Naseby's?' I suggest.

'That'll do. I've got an hour.'

The café has ambient music, low lighting, and cloth napkins. Keith wants a cappuccino, I want (another) Americano; he doesn't want a sandwich. He insists on paying. We find a booth with a SoundScreen at the back of the coffee shop, and sit down facing each other across the table.

He asks after my mother and my half-brother and half-sister, none of whom have sent greetings, though I pretend they have. We do some more catching up, and run out of small talk. Keith takes an e-cig from his pocket and sucks on it, sighs out vapour.

'Bad habit I picked up in the clink,' he says.

'No problem,' I say.

'Well,' he says. 'Here we are.'

'Yes,' I say.

'Why did you come? I mean, I'm grateful, happy to see you, but...' His voice trails off. He shrugs one shoulder. 'I don't understand why you'd want to see me.'

'Why didn't you write back?' I ask.

'I did,' he says.

'"Dear Conal, Please don't write to me any more about this, yours sincerely, Keith",' I quote back at him, derisively, accurately, and comprehensively.

He looks abashed. 'I didn't want you involved.'

'That was my choice.'

'Yes, when you were, what, fifteen? You have better things to do at that age. Your studies, for a start.'

'I did them,' I said. 'I'm doing all right. I'm starting at Glasgow

Uni in September.'

'Congratulations,' he says. A wry smile. 'Not law, I hope.'

'English.'

'Good, good.' He sucks hard on his nicotine stick. 'Speaking of law... I did read the documents you sent. You made quite a strong case – or at least, one that an actual lawyer could have turned into a sound basis for an appeal.'

'Why didn't you?' I ask. 'I showed... I showed...'

I can't go on.

'You showed the conviction wasn't safe,' says Keith. 'Well, as I say, you showed how a good brief could have shown it wasn't safe. And you were right.'

'I was?'

'Oh yes. Any number of other people could have done what I was accused of. If that line of defence had been taken in the first place, instead of that it could have been an accident... ' His gaze wanders. 'Who knows?'

'So why didn't you use what I found to appeal?'

'Go through all that just to get out a couple of years sooner? That's what it would have amounted to, at the most.'

'Two years might not matter to you,' I say. 'But they mattered to me. And you would have *cleared your name*. And I wouldn't have *wasted my time*.'

I'm not sure which of these burns more.

He gives me a lid-lowered look.

'I told you not to.'

'Look, Dad,' I find myself saying, rather to my surprise, 'I've found out much more since then. Look at this.'

I take out my phone and unfold it, spreading it out to a half-metre square on the table. I jiggle my finger across it, pulling up documents, highlighting, making connections in dotted and heavy lines.

'Harkins, Singh, McCulloch, right? All of them had the same access as you did. I haven't found anything on Harkins, but the other two –! Singh got his first degree in Kerala, and back then he was definitely involved in the peasant movement – arrested and interrogated on suspicion of terrorism –'

'Which he made no secret of,' Keith interjects. 'And he was released after a week, which in those days took some doing, I can tell you.'

'Yes – but whose doing? That's what I wonder. And then there's James McCulloch, the technician. Evangelical fundamentalist Christian; wrote endless screeds on his personal website and for the church magazine about how the variant texts of the scriptures were all forged by the Vatican and by various heretics and how the King James Version was based on the best manuscripts. He was a complete obsessive on the subject.'

Keith laughs. 'Not at work, he wasn't. Nice chap, scholarly. He worked as a technician to support his real calling, he said. But Jim was an excellent technician.' He peers closer at the spread-out screen. 'Dead now, I see. Shame. What's this got to do with anything?'

'Don't you see? Means, motive, opportunity! He had them all.'

Keith snorts. 'That's ridiculous! I remember him banging on about the Codex Vaticanus and the Codex Sinaiticus, and you know what? They're still intact, because they're on parchment, not paper. As McCulloch well knew! Only the very oldest fragments are on papyrus, and McCulloch rated them highly, as evidence of how early the New Testament was. So he didn't have any motive to release the Rot, even supposing he would do such a thing.'

'But –'

Keith leans back, shaking his head. 'Conal, you're young, you don't – now please don't take this the wrong way – you don't have much experience of people, or you wouldn't even think of that scenario. You have this prejudice of the fundamentalist as terrorist, as book-burner. No. That's not how it was, and it wasn't how Jim was. As for Dr Singh…' He shakes his head, again. 'You can go and meet him, you know that? He's a Head of Department now, still at Strathclyde University, probably sitting in his office right this minute, not five hundred metres away.' He takes out his phone. 'Want me to call him?'

'No, no, no need,' I say, hastily, taken aback. Somehow I hadn't thought of my suspects as real, as living rather than as shadowy, reconstructed figures in my mind.

'I thought not,' says Keith. He puts away the phone. 'Look, Conal, I understand why you're doing this. I appreciate it. It does you credit. But it's not going to help me, or you. Because…' He takes a deep breath. 'I've never said this before. I'll never say it again. But I *know* these guys were innocent, because *I did it.*'

For a moment, it's like there's been a power-supply glitch and an earth tremor. I press my hands on the edge of the table. My mouth is dry.

'And it wasn't an accident,' he adds.

I'm feeling nauseous. There have been worse crimes, but none worse or more consequential was ever committed by one person acting alone. Set aside the deaths: I know these are almost all indirect, statistical, speculative, and disputable. Think about the books, the documents, the letters, the photographs, the notes, the archives… all gone to dust because of the Rot. So many things we'll never know, now. So many questions that'll never be settled.

I have only one question left.

'Why?'

He puffs on the e-cig. 'It had to be done. History was killing us – or rather, we were killing each other over history. Every day I got the train in from Dumbarton, and walked through this

95

station and up the road to the university, and every week there'd be a bomb scare. If it wasn't one lot it was another. Islamists, Irish dissidents, the bloody Prods even. And one day I realised that every one of them had been brought up on some version of history -'

'Oral history! Songs and stories. Isn't that enough for these people? And radical websites! So what –?'

Keith shakes his head. 'No, in the long run they need written history. Behind every cause you'll find historians. Bloody archive rats. But without the authority of original documents, every text becomes shit someone said on the internet. And the songs: the songs become fiddle-de-de. I mean, do you know where the fields of Athenry even *were*? That day, I looked up at the station roof – it was new, then – and thought, that's what we need! The surface of last scattering, a time you can't look farther back than. A clean break, a new start. A new beginning of history. And I realised I had exactly what was needed, in the GM fungi we were working on to recycle paper. Just a few tweaks to the genome, that's all it would take.' He folds his finger-tips back to his thumb, flicks them out, blows. 'A handful of spores on the wind, from the roof of the building. That's how I did it.'

'Why didn't you plead guilty?'

He shrugs. 'I thought maybe I could get off, that they couldn't pin it on me, but I didn't want to *lie* about anything. So I said nothing. I let the lawyer come up with the best defence he could. Not good enough, as it turned out.'

'Jesus.' I stare at him, still feeling sick. 'How could you...?'

'I've often asked myself that,' he says. 'And I know I've messed up your life, and Clara's, but... the truth is – I was thinking of the world you were going to grow up in. I was thinking of you.'

My fists clench. 'Don't bring me into it!'

'It's not an excuse. But face it, Conal. It's not such a bad world, now. We look to the future, not the past. Speaking of which...' He glances at his watch. 'I have a train to catch, and a plane.'

'Where to?' I ask, numbed to idle curiosity.

'Far away,' he says. 'The Arctic, if you must know. I got a job on the rigs.' He stands, slaps my shoulder. 'Keep in touch.'

He goes out, the rolling case trundling behind him. I think of running after him, of demanding more explanation or apology, and I think better of it. After a while I get up and go out of the dim clattering café to the bright busy concourse. In a few minutes it's going to be even busier. Trains whose journey started in Paris, or Shanghai, or Cape Town are coming in. I walk to a dead alcove between the toilet entrance and the Burger King, face into the wall, and take the old laminated photo from my inside jacket pocket. From my trouser pocket I take a penknife, and open it.

'Don't do it,' says a voice behind me.

I turn. It's the girl who spoke to me earlier. She's looking at me with concern.

'I wasn't going to slit my wrist or anything,' I say. I show her my hands, with the knife and the picture. 'I was just going to cut this open.'

'I know,' she says. She lays a hand on my arm. 'I guessed... your dad was in prison a long time. I knew you'd be upset after meeting him. So I kept an eye out for you. He's gone now. You don't have to do that. No matter what he did, that moment happened. He must have had some goodness in him then, you can see it on his face. You should keep it.'

'You're right,' I say, 'except... he was always a good man. He still is. And that's why I'm doing this.'

Moving slowly and carefully, I prick the laminated surface with the tip of the blade, and slice along the edges, then peel back the plastic. Within seconds, the first tiny black spot has appeared, as one of the invisible, omnipresent spores of the Rot settles and begins its work. Within an hour, the whole picture will be dust.

The next moment, and without my being able to stop her, the girl has flashed her phone over my hand, and taken a picture of the picture.

'Just in case you change your mind,' she says.

I frown at her, shaking my head. 'I won't,' I say, 'but, if I did, how would I find you?'

'Do you ever get the feeling,' she says, 'that there are times when you're really stupid?'

'Yes,' I say.

She nods. 'This is one of them,' she says. 'And I expect I'll remind you of it, often, in the future.'

'You seem very confident about the future.'

'Oh yes,' she says. 'I am. Let's find out.'

I drop the paper and plastic and walk with her out of the station, not looking back.

The Vorkuta Event

1. Tentacles and Tomes

It was in 19–, that unforgettable year, that I first believed I had
unearthed the secret cause of the guilt and shame that so
evidently burdened Dr David Rigley Walker, Emeritus Professor
of Zoology at the University of G------. The occasion was casual
enough. A module of the advanced class in zoology dealt with the
philosophical and historical aspects of the science. I had been
assigned to write an essay on the history of our subject, with
especial reference to the then not quite discredited notion of the
inheritance of acquired characteristics. Most of my fellow
students, of a more practical cast of mind than my own, were
inclined to regard this as an irrelevant chore. Not I.

With the arrogance of youth, I believed that our subject,
zoology, had the potential to assimilate a much wider field of
knowledge than its current practice and exposition was inclined
to assume. Is not Man an animal? Is not, therefore, all that is
human within, in principle, the scope of zoology? Such, at least,
was my reasoning at the time, and my excuse for a wide and – in
mature retrospect – less than profitable reading. Certain recent
notorious and lucrative popularisations – as well as serious
studies of sexual and social behaviour, pioneered by, of all people,
entomologists – were in my view a mere glimpse of the empire of
thought open to the zoologist. In those days such fields as
evolutionary psychology, Darwinian medicine and ecological
economics still struggled in the shattered and noisome eggshell of

their intellectually and – more importantly – militarily crushed progenitors. The great reversal of the mid-century's verdict on this and other matters still slumbered in the womb of the future. These were, I may say, strange times, a moment of turbulent transition when the molecular doctrines were already established, but before they had become the very basis of biology. In the minds of older teachers and in the pages of obsolete textbooks certain questions now incontrovertible seemed novel and untried. The ghost of vitalism still walked the seminar room; plate tectonics was solid ground mainly to geologists; notions of intercontinental land bridges, and even fabled Lemuria, had not been altogether dispelled as worthy of at least serious dismissal. I deplored – nay, detested – all such vagaries.

So it was with a certain zeal, I confess, that I embarked on the background reading for my modest composition. I walked into the University library at noon, bounded up the stairs to the science floor, and alternated browsing the stacks and scribbling in my carrel for a good five hours. Unlike some of my colleagues, I had not afflicted myself with the nicotine vice, and was able to proceed uninterrupted save for a call of nature. I delved into Lamarck himself, in verbose Victorian translation; into successive editions of *The Origin of Species*; and into the *Journal of the History of Biology*. I had already encountered Koestler's *The Case of the Midwife Toad*, that devastating but regretful demolition of the Lamarckian claims of the fellow-travelling biologist, fraud, and suicide Viktor Kammerer – the book, in well-thumbed paperback, was an underground classic among zoology undergraduates, alongside Lyall Watson's *Supernature*. I read and wrote with a fury to discredit, for good and all, the long-exploded hypothesis that was the matter of my essay. But when I had completed the notes and outline, and the essay was as good as written, needing only some connecting phrases and a fair copy, a sense that the task was not quite finished nagged.

I leaned back in the plastic seat, and recollected of a sudden the very book I needed to deliver the *coup de grace*. But where had I seen it? I could almost smell it – and it was the sense of smell that brought back the memory of the volume's location. I stuffed my notes in a duffel bag, placed my stack of borrowings on the Returns trolley, and hurried from the library. Late in the autumn term, late in the day, the University's central building, facing me on the same hilltop as the tall and modern library, loomed black like a gothic mansion against the sunset sky. Against the same sky, bare trees stood like preparations of nerve-endings on an iodine-stained slide. I crossed the road and walked around the side of the edifice and down the slope to the Zoology Department, a sandstone and glass monument to the 1920s. Within: paved floors, tiled walls and hardwood balustrades, and the smell that had reminded me, a mingled pervasive waft of salt-water aquaria, of rat and rabbit droppings, of disinfectant and of beeswax polish. A porter smoked in his den, recognised me with a brief incurious glance. I nodded, turned and ascended the broad stone staircase. On the first landing a portrait of Darwin overhung the door to the top of the lecture hall; beneath the window lay a long glass case containing a dusty plastic model of *Architeuthys*, its two-metre tentacles outstretched to a painted prey. The scale of the model was not specified. At the top of the stairs, opposite the entrance to the library, stood another glass case, with the skeleton of a specimen of *Canis dirus* from Rancho La Brea. As I moved, the shadow and gleams of the dire wolf's teeth presented a lifelike snarl.

Inside, the departmental library was empty, its long windows catching the sun's last light. From the great table that occupied most of its space, the smell of beeswax rose like a hum, drowning out the air's less salubrious notes save that of the books that lined the walls. Here I had skimmed Schrödinger's neglected text on the nerves; here I had luxuriated in D'Arcy Thomson's glorious prose, the outpoured, ecstatic precision of *On Growth and Form*; here, more productively, I had bent until my eyes had watered over Mayr and Simpson and Dobzhansky. It was the last, I think, who had first sent me to glance, with a shudder, at the book I now sought.

There it was, black and thick as a Bible; its binding sturdy, its pages yellowing but sound, like a fine vellum. *The Situation in Biological Science: Proceedings of the Lenin Academy of Agricultural Sciences of the U.S.S.R., July 31 – August 7, 1948, Complete Stenographic Report*. This verbatim account is one of the most sinister in the annals of science: it documents the conference at which the peasant charlatan Lysenko, who claimed that the genetic constitutions of organisms could be changed by environmental influences, defeated those of his opponents who still stood up for Mendelian genetics. Genetics in the Soviet Union took decades to recover.

I took the volume to the table, sat down and copied to my notebook Lysenko's infamous, gloating remark toward the close of the conference: 'The Central Committee of the CPSU has examined my report and approved it'; and a selection from the rush of hasty recantations – announcements, mostly, of an overnight repudiation of a lifetime's study – that followed it and preceded the closing vote of thanks to Stalin. I felt pleased at having found – unfairly perhaps – something with which to sully further the heritage of Lamarck. At the same time I felt an urge to wash my hands. There was something incomprehensible about the book's very existence: was it naivety or arrogance that made its publishers betray so shameful a demonstration of the political control of science? The charlatan's empty victory was a thing that deserved to be done in the dark, not celebrated in a *complete stenographic report.*

But enough. As I stood to return the book to the shelf I opened it idly at the flyleaf, and noticed a queer thing. The sticker proclaiming it the property of the Department overlaid a handwritten inscription in broad black ink, the edges of which scrawl had escaped the bookplate's obliteration. I recognised some of the fugitive lettering as Cyrillic script. Curious, I held the book up to the light and tried to read through the page, but the paper was too thick.

The books were for reference only. The rule was strict. I was alone in the library. I put the book in my duffel bag and carried it to my bedsit. There, with an electric kettle on a shaky table, I steamed the bookplate off. Then, cribbing from a battered second-hand copy of *The Penguin Russian Course*, I deciphered the inscription. The Russian original has faded from my mind. The translation remains indelible:

> *To my dear friend Dr. Dav. R. Walker,*
> *in memory of our common endeavour,*
> *yours,*
> *Ac. T. D. Lysenko.*

The feeling that this induced in me may be imagined. I started and trembled as though something monstrous had reached out a clammy tentacle from the darkness of its lair and touched the back of my neck. If the book had been inscribed to any other academic elder I might have been less shocked: many of them flaunted their liberal views, and hinted at an earlier radicalism, on the rare occasions when politics were discussed; but Walker was a true-blue conservative of the deepest dye, as well as a mathematically rigorous Darwinian.

The next morning I trawled the second-hand bookshops of

the University district. The city had a long, though now mercifully diminishing, 'Red' tradition; and sure enough, I found crumbling pamphlets and tedious journals of that persuasion from the time of the Lysenko affair. In them I found articles defending Lysenko's views. The authors of some, the translators of others, variously appeared as: DRW, Dr D R Walker, and (with a more proletarian swagger) Dave Walker. There was no room for doubt: my esteemed professor had been a Lysenkoist in his youth.

With a certain malice (forgivable in view of my shock and indeed dismay) I made a point of including these articles in my references when I typed up the essay and handed it in to my tutor, Dr F------. A week passed before I received a summons to Professor Walker's office.

2. Alcohol, Tobacco, and Ultraviolet Radiation Exposure

The Emeritus Professor was, as his title suggests, semi-retired; he took little part in the administration, and devoted his intermittent visits to the Department to the occasional sparkling but well-worn lecture; to shuffling and annotating off-prints of papers from his more productive days with a view to an eventual collection; and to some desultory research of his own into the anatomy and relationships of a Jurassic marine crocodile. Palaeontology had been his field. In his day he had led expeditions to the Kalahari and the Gobi. He had served in the Second World War. In some biographical note I had glimpsed the rank of Lieutenant, but no reference to the Service in which it had been attained: a matter on which rumour had not been reticent.

The professor's office was at the end of one of the second storey's long corridors. Dust, cobwebs, and a statistically significant sample of desiccated invertebrates begrimed the frosted glass panel of the door. I tapped, dislodging a dead spider and a couple of woodlice.

'Come in!'

As I stepped through the door the professor rose behind his desk and leaned forward. Tall and stooping, very thin, with weathered skin, sunken cheeks and a steely spade of beard, he seemed a ruin of his adventurous youth – more Quatermass than Quatermain, so to speak – but an impressive ruin. He shook hands across his desk, motioned me to a seat, and resumed his own. I brushed tobacco ash from friction-furred leather and sat down. The room reeked of pipe smoke and of an acetone whiff that might have been formaldehyde or whisky breath. Shelves lined the walls, stacked with books and petrified bones. Great drifts of journals and off-prints cluttered the floor. A window overlooking the building's drab courtyard sifted wan wintry light through a patina similar to that on the door. A fluorescent tube and an Anglepoise diminished even that effect of daylight.

Walker leaned back in his chair and flicked a Zippo over the bowl of his Peterson. He tapped a yellow forefinger-nail on a sheaf of paper, which I recognised without surprise as my essay.

'Well, Cameron,' he said, through a grey-blue cloud, 'you've done your homework.'

'Thank you, sir,' I said.

He jabbed the pipe-stem at me. 'You're not at school,' he said. 'That is no way for one gentleman to address another.'

'Okay, Walker,' I said, a little too lightly.

'Not,' he went on, 'that your little trick here was gentlemanly. You're expected to cite peer-reviewed articles, not dredge up political squibs and screeds from what you seized on as another chap's youthful folly. These idiocies are no secret. If you'd asked me, I'd have told you all about them – the circumstances, you understand. And I could have pointed you to the later peer-reviewed article in which I tore these idiocies, which I claimed as my own, to shreds. You could have cited that too. That would have been polite.'

'I didn't intend any discourtesy,' I said.

'You intended to embarrass me,' he said. 'Did you not?'

I found myself scratching the back of my head, embarrassed myself. My attempt at an excuse came out as an accusation.

'I found the inscription from Lysenko,' I said.

Walker rocked back in his seat. 'What?'

'"To my dear friend Dr David R Walker, in memory of our common endeavour".' Against my conscious will, the words came out in a jeering tone.

Walker planted his elbow-patches on his desk and cupped his chin in both hands, pipe jutting from his yellow teeth. He glared at me through a series of puffs.

'Ah, yes,' he said at last. 'That common endeavour. Would it perhaps pique your curiosity to know what it *was*?'

'I had assumed it was on genetics,' I said.

'Hah!' snorted Walker. 'You're a worse fool than I was, Cameron. What could I have done on genetics?'

'You wrote about it,' I said, again sounding more accusing than I had meant to.

'I wrote rubbish for *The Modern Quarterly*,' he said, 'but I think you would be hard pressed to find in it anything about original work on genetics.'

'I mean,' I said, 'your defence of him.'

Walker narrowed his eyes. 'These articles were written *after* I had received the book,' he said. 'So they were not what old Trofim was remembering me for, no indeed.'

'So what was it?'

He straightened up. 'A most disquieting experience,' he said. 'One that weighs on me even now. If I were to tell you of it, it would weigh on you for the rest of your life. And the strange thing is, Cameron, that I need not swear you to secrecy. The tale is as unbelievable as it is horrible. For you to tell it would merely destroy whatever credibility you have. Not only would nobody believe the tale – nobody would believe that I had told it to you. The more you insisted on it, the more you would brand yourself a liar and a fantasist of the first water.'

'Then why should I believe it myself?'

His parchment skin and tombstone teeth grinned back his answer like a death's head illuminated from within.

'You will believe it.'

I shrugged.

'You will wish you didn't,' he added mildly. 'You can walk out that door and forget about this, and I will forget your little jape. If you don't, if you stay here and listen to me, let me assure you that I will have inflicted upon you a most satisfactory revenge.'

I squared to him from my seat. 'Try me, Walker,' I said.

3. Walker's Account

Stalin's pipe was unlit – always a bad sign. Poskrebyshev, the General Secretary's sepulchral amanuensis, closed the door silently behind me. The only pool of light in the long, thickly curtained room was over Stalin's desk. Outside that pool two figures sat on high-backed chairs. A double glint on pinz-nez was enough to warn me that one of these figures was Beria. The other, as I approached, I identified at once by his black flop of hair, his hollow cheeks, and his bright fanatic eyes: Trofim Lysenko. My knees felt like rubber. I had met Stalin before, of course, during the war, but I had never been summoned to his presence.

It was the summer of '47. I'd been kicking my heels in Moscow for weeks, trying without success – and more frustratingly, without definite refusal – to get permission to mount another expedition to the Gobi. It was not, of course, the best of times to be a British citizen in the Soviet capital. (It was not the best of times to be a Soviet citizen, come to that.) My wartime work in liaison may have been both a positive and a negative factor: positive, in that I had contacts, and a degree of respect; negative, in that it put me under suspicion – ludicrous though it may seem, Cameron – of being a spy. I might, like so many others, have gone straight from the Kremlin to the Lubianka.

Stalin rose, stalked towards me, shook hands brusquely, pointed me to a low seat – he was notoriously sensitive about his height – and returned to his desk chair. I observed him closely but covertly. He had lost weight. His skin was loose. He seemed more burdened than he had at Yalta and Tehran.

'Lieutenant Walker –' he began. Then he paused, favoured me with a yellow-eyed, yellow-toothed smile, and corrected himself. '*Doctor* Walker. Rest assured, you were not invited here in your capacity as a British officer.'

His sidelong glance at Beria told me all I needed to know about where I stood in that regard. Stalin sucked on his empty pipe, frowned, and fumbled a packet of Dunhills from his tunic. To my surprise, he proffered the pack across the desk. I took one, with fingers that barely trembled. A match flared between us; and for a moment, in that light, I saw that Stalin was afraid. He was more afraid than I; and that thought terrified me. I sank back and drew hard.

'We need your help, Dr Walker. In a scientific capacity.'

I hesitated, unsure how to address him. He was no comrade of mine, and to call him by his latest title, 'Generalissimo', would have seemed fawning. My small diplomatic experience came to my aid.

'You surprise me, Marshal Stalin,' I said. 'My Soviet colleagues are more than capable.'

Lysenko cleared his throat, but it was Beria who spoke. 'Let us say there are problems.'

'It is not,' said Stalin, 'a question of capability. It is important to us that the task we wish you to take part in be accomplished by a British scientist who is also a... former... British officer, who has – let us say – certain connections with certain services, and who is not – again, let us say – one who might, at some future date, be suspected of being connected with the organs of Soviet state security.' Another sidelong glance at Beria.

'Let me be blunt, Marshal Stalin,' I said. 'You want me because I'm a scientist and because you think I might be a British agent, and because you can be certain I'm not one of yours?'

'Fairly certain,' said Stalin, with a dark chuckle.

Out of the corner of my eye I saw Beria flinch. I was startled that Stalin should hint so broadly of Soviet penetration of British intelligence, as well as of his mistrust of Beria. If I survived to return to England, I would make a point of reporting it directly to that chap who – Whitehall rumour had it – was in charge of stopping that sort of thing. What was his name again? Oh, yes – Philby. A moment later I realised that, very likely, Stalin and Beria had cooked up this apparent indiscretion between them, perhaps to test my reaction, or so that my very reporting of it might circuitously advance their sinister aims. But there were more pressing puzzles on my mind.

'But I'm a palaeontologist!' I said. 'What could there possibly be in that field that could be of interest to any intelligence service?'

'A good question,' said Stalin. 'An intriguing question, is it not? I see you are intrigued. All I can say at this point, Dr Walker, is that you have only one way of finding the answer. If you choose not to help us, then I must say, with regret, that you must take the next flight for London. It may be impossible for you to return, or to dig again for the dinosaur bones of Outer Mongolia which appear to fascinate you so much. If you do choose to help us, not only will you find the answer to your question, but opportunities for further collaboration with our scientists might, one may imagine, open up.'

The threat, mercifully small as it would have seemed to some, was dire to me; the offer tempting; but neither was necessary. I was indeed intrigued.

'I'll do it,' I said.

'Good,' said Stalin. 'I now turn you over to the capable hands of...'

He paused just long enough – a heartbeat – to scare me.

'...your esteemed colleague, Trofim Denisovich.'

But, as though in amends for that small, cat-like moment of sporting with my fear, or perhaps from that sentimental streak which so often characterises his type, his parting handshake was accompanied by momentary wetness of his yellow eyes and a confidential murmur, the oddest thing I ever heard – or heard of or read of – him say:

'God go with you.'

Corridors, guards, stairs, the courtyard, more guards, then Red Square and the streets. Trofim walked quickly beside me, hands jammed in his jacket pockets, his chin down; fifty-odd metres behind us, the pacing shadow of the man from the organs of state security. Beefy-faced women in kerchiefs mixed concrete by shovel, struggled with wheel-barrows, took bawled orders from loutish foremen. Above them, on the bare scaffolding of the building sites, huge red-bordered black-on-white banners flapped, vast magnifications of a flattering ink portrait of the face I had seen minutes before. There seemed to be no connection, the merest passing resemblance to the aged, pock-marked man. I recalled something he had, it was told, once snarled at his drunken, vainglorious son, who'd pleaded, 'After all, I too am Stalin.' He'd said: '*You* are not Stalin! *I* am not Stalin! Stalin is a banner...'

At that moment I thought I could quite literally see what he'd meant.

'Well, David Rigley,' said Lysenko (evidently under the misapprehension that my second name was a patronymic), 'the leading comrades have landed you and me in a fine mess.'

'You know what this is about?'

'I do, more's the pity. We may be doomed men. Let us walk a little. It's the safest way to talk.'

'But surely –'

'Nothing is "surely", here. You must know that. Even a direct order from the Boss may not be enough to protect us from the organs. Beria is building atomic bombs out on the tundra. Where he gets his labour force from, you can guess. Including engineers and scientists, alas. At one of their sites they have found something that... they want us to look into.'

'Atomic bombs? With respect, Trofim Denisovich –'

'I will not argue with you on that. But what Beria's... men have found is more terrifying than an atomic bomb. That is what we have agreed to investigate, you and I.'

'Oh,' I said. 'So that's what I've agreed to. Thanks for clearing that up.'

The sarcasm was wasted on him.

'You are welcome, David Rigley.' He stopped at an intersection. A black car drew up beside us. He waved me to the side door. I hung back.

'It is my own car,' he said mildly. 'It will take us to my farm. Tomorrow, it will take us to the airport.'

Lysenko's private collective farm – so to speak – in the Gorki-Leninskie hills south of Moscow was of course a showcase, and was certainly a testimony more to Lysenko's enthusiasm than to his rigour, but I must admit that it was a hospitable place, and that I spent a pleasant enough afternoon there being shown its remarkable experiments, and a very pleasant evening eating some of the results. For that night, Trofim and I could pretend to have not a care in the world – and in that pretence alone, I was of one mind with the charlatan.

The following morning we flew to the east and north. It was not a civilian flight. Aeroflot's reputation is deservedly bad enough; but it is in the armed forces that Aeroflot pilots learn their trade. This flight in an LI-2 transport was courtesy of the Army. Even now, the memory of that flight brings me out in a cold sweat. So you will forgive me if I pass over it. Suffice to say that we touched down on a remote military airfield that evening to refuel and to change pilots, and continued through a night during which I think I slept in my cramped bucket seat from sheer despair. We landed – by sideslip and steep, tight spiral, as if under fire – just after dawn the following morning on a bumpy, unpaved strip in the midst of a flat, green plain. A shack served as a terminal building, before which a welcoming committee of a dozen or so uniformed men stood. Through a small porthole, as the plane juddered to a halt, I glimpsed some more distant structures: a tower on stilts, long low barracks, a mine-head, and great heaps of spoil. There may have been a railway line. I'm not sure.

Trofim and I unkinked our backs, rubbed grit from our eyes, and made our stooping way to the hatch. I jumped the metre drop to the ground. Trofim sat and swung his long legs over and slid off more carefully. The air was fine and fresh, unbelievably so after Moscow, and quite warm. One of the men detached himself from the lineup and hurried over. He was stocky, blue-jowled, with a look of forced joviality on his chubby, deep-lined face. He wore a cap with the deep blue band of the security organs. Shaking hands, he introduced himself as Colonel Viktor A. Marchenko. He led us to the shack, where he gave us glasses of tea and chunks of sour black bread, accompanied by small talk and no information, while his men remained at attention outside – they didn't smoke or shuffle – then took us around the back of the shack to a Studebaker flat-bed truck. To my surprise, the colonel took the driver's seat. Trofim and I squeezed in beside him. The rest of the unit piled perilously on the back.

We associate Russia's far north with snow and ice. Its brief summer is almost pleasant, apart from the mosquitoes and the landslides. Small flowers carpet the tundra. Its flat appearance is deceptive, concealing from a distance the many hollows and rises of the landscape. The truck went up and down, its tyres chewing the unstable soil. At the crest of each successive rise the distant buildings loomed closer. The early morning sun glinted on long horizontal lines in front of them: barbed wire, no doubt, and not yet rusty. It became obvious, as I had of course suspected, that this was a labour camp. I looked at Lysenko. He stared straight ahead, sweat beading his face. I braced my legs in the foot-well and gripped my knees hard.

At the top of a rise the truck halted. The colonel nodded forward, and made a helpless gesture with his hand. Trofim and I stared in shock at what lay in front of us. At the bottom of the declivity, just a few metres down the grassy slope from the nose of the truck, the ground seemed to have given way. The hole was about fifteen metres across and four deep. Scores of brown corpses, contorted and skeletal, protruded at all angles from the ragged black earth. From the bottom of the hole, an edged metallic point stood up like the tip of a pyramid or the corner of an enormous box. Not a speck of dirt marred the reflective sheen of its blue-tinted, silvery surfaces.

My first thought was that some experimental device, perhaps one of Beria's atomic bombs, had crashed here among some of the camp's occupants, killing and half-burying the poor fellows. My second thought was that it had exposed the mass grave of an earlier batch of similar unfortunates. I kept these thoughts to myself and stepped down from the cab, followed by Lysenko. The colonel jumped out the other side and barked an order. Within seconds his men had formed a widely-spaced cordon around the hole, each standing well back, with his Kalashnikov levelled.

'Take a walk around it,' said Marchenko.

We did, keeping a few steps away from the raw edge of the circular gash. About three metres of each edge of the object was exposed. Lysenko stopped and walked to the brink. I followed, to peer at a corpse just below our feet. Head, torso and one outflung arm poked out of the soil. Leathery skin, a tuft of hair, empty sockets and a lipless grin.

'From the... *Yezhovschina?*' I asked, alluding to the massacres of a decade earlier.

Trofim leaned forward and pointed down. 'I doubt,' he said drily, 'that any such died with bronze swords in their hands.'

I squatted and examined the body more closely. Almost hidden by a fall of dirt was the other hand, clutching a hilt that did indeed, between the threads of a rotten tassel, have a brassy gleam. I looked again at what shock had made me overlook on the others: stubs of blades, scraps of gear, leather belts and studs, here and there around withered necks a torc of a dull metal that might have been pewter.

'So who are they?' I asked.

Lysenko shrugged. 'Tartars, Mongols...'

His knowledge of history was more dubious than his biology. These peoples had never migrated so far north, and no Bronze Age people was native to the area. The identity and origin of the dead barbarians puzzles me to this day.

Around the other side of the pit, the side that faced the camp, things were very different. The upper two metres of that face of the pyramid was missing, as if it was the opened top of that hypothetical box's corner. And the bodies – I counted ten – scattered before it were definitely those of camp labourers: thin men in thin clothes, among flung shovels. The corpses looked quite fresh. Only their terrible rictus faces were like those of the other and more ancient dead.

'What is this?' I asked Lysenko. 'One of Beria's infernal machines?'

He shot me an amused, impatient glance. 'You overestimate us,' he said. 'This is not a product of our technology. Nor, I venture to suggest, is it one of yours.'

'Then whose?'

'If it is not from some lost civilisation of deep antiquity, then it is not of this world.'

We gazed for a while at the black empty triangle and then completed our circuit of the pit and returned to Marchenko, who still stood in front of the truck.

'What happened here?' Lysenko asked.

Marchenko pointed towards the camp, then down at the ground.

'This is a mining camp,' he said. 'The mine's galleries extend beneath our feet. Some days ago, there was a cave-in. It resulted in a rapid subsidence on the surface, and exposed the object, and the slain warriors. A small squad of prisoners was sent into the pit to investigate, and to dig out the bodies and artefacts. To be quite frank, I suspect that they were sent to dig for valuables, gold and what not. One of them, for reasons we can only speculate, tried to enter the aperture in the object. Within moments, they were all dead.'

'Tell us plainly,' said Lysenko. 'Do you mean they were shot by the guards?'

The colonel shook his head. 'They could have been,' he said, 'for disobeying orders. But as it happens, they were not. Something from the object killed them without leaving a mark. Perhaps a poisonous gas – I don't know. That is for you to find out.'

His story struck as improbable, or at least incomplete, but this was no time to dispute it.

'For heaven's sake, man!' I cried out. 'And get killed ourselves?'

Marchenko bared a gold incisor. 'That is the problem, yes? You are scientists. Solve it.'

This insouciance for a moment infuriated us, but solve it we did. An hour or two later, after the truck had returned from the camp with the simple equipment we'd demanded, Lysenko and I were standing in the pit a couple of metres from the black aperture. Behind us the truck chugged, its engine powering a searchlight aimed at the dark triangle. Trofim guided a long pole, on the end of which one of the truck's wing mirrors was lashed. I stood in front of him, the pole resting on my shoulder, and peered at the mirror with a pair of binoculars requisitioned from (no doubt) a camp guard. Nothing happened as our crude apparatus inched above the dark threshold. We moved about, Trofim turning the mirror this way and that. The magnified mirror image filled a large part of the close-focus view.

'What do you see?' Lysenko asked.

'Nothing,' I said. 'Well, the joins of the edges. They go as far as I can see. Below it there's just darkness. It's very deep.'

We backed out and scrambled up.

'How big is this thing?' I asked Marchenko.

He shifted and looked sideways, then jabbed a finger downward.

'A similar apex,' he said, 'pokes down into the gallery beneath us.'

'How far beneath us?'

His tongue flicked between his lips for a moment. 'About a hundred metres.'

'If this is a cube,' I said, 'four hundred feet diagonally – my God!'

'We have reason to think it is a cube,' said Marchenko.

'Take us to the lower apex,' said Lysenko.

'Do you agree?' Marchenko asked me.

'Yes,' I said.

A sign arched over the camp entrance read: 'Work in the USSR is a matter of honour and glory'. For all that we could see as the truck drove in, nobody in the camp sought honour and glory that day. Guards stood outside every barracks door. Three scrawny men were summoned to work the hoist. Marchenko's squad took up positions around the mine-head. Lysenko, Marchenko and I – with one of Marchenko's sergeants carrying the pole and mirror – descended the shaft in a lift cage to the gallery. Pitchblende glittered in the beams from our helmet lamps. We walked forward for what seemed like many hours, but according to my watch was only fifty-five minutes. The cave-in had been cleared. Down like the point of a dagger came the lower apex of the cube, its tip a few inches above the floor. Its open face was not black but bright. It cast a blue light along the cavern.

'Well,' said Lysenko, with a forced laugh, 'this looks more promising.'

This time it was I who advanced with the pole and angled the mirror in; Lysenko who looked through the Zeiss. I saw a reflected flash, as though something had moved inside the object. Blue light, strangely delimited, strangely slow, like some luminous fluid, licked along the wooden pole. With a half-second's warning, I could have dropped it. But as that gelid lightning flowed over my hands, my fingers clamped to the wood. I felt a forward tug. I could not let go. My whole body spasmed as if in electric shock, and just as painfully. My feet rose off the ground, and my legs kicked out behind me. At the same moment I found myself flying forward like a witch clinging to a wayward broom. With a sudden flexure that almost cracked my spine, I was jerked through the inverted triangular aperture and upward into the blue-lit space above. That space was not empty. Great blocks of blue, distinct but curiously insubstantial, floated about me. I was borne upwards, then brought to a halt. I could see, far above, a small triangle of daylight, in equally vivid contrast to the darkness immediately beneath it and the unnatural light around me. Apart from my hands, still clutched around the pole, my muscles returned to voluntary control. I hung there, staring, mouth open, writhing like a fish on a hook. My throat felt raw, my gasps sounded ragged. I realised that I had been screaming. The echoes of my screams rang for a second or two in the vast cubical space.

Before my eyes, some of the blocky shapes took on a new arrangement: a cubist caricature of a human face, in every detail down to the teeth. Eyes like cogwheels, ears like coffins. From somewhere came an impression, nay, a conviction, that this representation was meant to be *reassuring*. It was not.

What happened next is as difficult to describe as a half-remembered dream: a sound of pictures, a taste of words. I had a vision of freezing space, of burning suns, of infinite blackness shot through with stars that were not eternal: stars that I might outlive. I heard the clash of an enormous conflict, remote in origin, endless in prospect, and pointless in issue. It was not a war of ideals, but an ideal war: what Plato might have called the Form of War. Our wars of interests and ideologies can give only the faintest foretaste of it. But a foretaste they are. I was given to understand – how, I do not know – that joining in such a war is what the future holds for our descendants, and for all intelligent species. It is conducted by machines that carry in themselves the memories, and are themselves the only monuments, of the races that built them and that they have subsumed. This is a war with infinite casualties, infinite woundings, and no death that is not followed – after no matter what lapse of time – by a resurrection and a further plunge into that unending welter. No death save that of the universe itself can release the combatants, and only at that terminus will it have meaning, and then only for a moment, the infinitesimal moment of contemplating a victory that is final because it precedes, by that infinitesimal moment, the end of all things: victory pure and undefiled, victory for its own sake, the victory of the last mind left.

This hellish vision was held out to me as an inducement! Yes, Cameron – I was being offered the rare and unthinkable privilege of joining the ranks of warriors in this conflict that even now shakes the universe; of joining it centuries or millennia before the human race rises to that challenge itself. I would join it as a mind: my brain patterns copied and transmitted across space to some fearsome new embodiment, my present body discarded as a husk. And if I refused, I would be cast aside with contempt. The picture that came before me – whether from my own mind, or from that of the bizarre visage before me – was of the scattered bodies in the pit.

With every fibre of my being, and regardless of consequence, I screamed my refusal. Death itself was infinitely preferable to that infinite conflict.

I was pulled upward so violently that my arms almost dislocated. The blue light faded, blackness enveloped me, and then the bright triangle loomed. I hurtled through it and fell with great force, face down in the mud. The wind was knocked out of me. I gasped, choked, and lifted my head painfully up, to find myself staring into the sightless eyes of one of the recent dead, the camp labourers. I screamed again, scrambled to my feet, and clawed my way up the crumbling side of the pit. For a minute I stood quite alone.

Then another body hurtled from the aperture, and behaved exactly as I had done, including the scream. But Lysenko had my outstretched hand to grasp his wrist as he struggled up.

'Were you pulled in after me?' I asked.

Lysenko shook his head. 'I rushed to try to pull you back.'

'You're a brave man,' I said.

He shrugged. 'Not brave enough for what I found in there.'

'You saw it?' I asked.

'Yes,' he said. He shuddered. 'Before that Valhalla, I would choose the hell of the priests.'

'What we saw,' I said, 'is entirely compatible with materialism. That's what's so terrifying.'

Lysenko clutched at my lapels. 'No, not materialism! Mechanism! Man must fight that!'

'Fight it... endlessly?'

His lips narrowed. He turned away.

'Marchenko lied to us,' he said.

'What?'

Lysenko nodded downward at the nearest bodies. 'That tale of his – these men were not sent into this pit here, and killed by something lashing out from the... device. These men are *miners*. They entered it exactly as we did, from below.'

'So why are they dead, and we're alive?' As soon as I asked the question, I knew the answer. Only their bodies were dead. Their minds were on their way to becoming alive somewhere else.

'You remember the choice you were given,' said Lysenko. 'They chose differently.'

'They chose *that* – over –?' I jerked a backward thumb.

'Yes,' said Lysenko. 'A different hell.'

We waited. After a while the truck returned from the camp.

4. Fallout Patterns

Walker fell silent in the lengthened shadows and thickened smoke.

'And then what happened?' I asked.

He knocked out his pipe. 'Nothing,' he said. 'Truck, plane, Moscow, Aeroflot, London. My feet barely touched the ground. I never went back.'

'I mean, what happened to the thing you found?'

'A year or two later, the site was used for an atomic test.'

'Over a uranium mine?'

'I believe that was part of the object. To maximise fallout. That particular region is still off limits, I understand.'

'How do you know this?'

'You should know better than to ask,' said Walker.

'So Stalin had your number!'

He frowned. 'What do you mean?'

'He guessed correctly,' I said. 'About your connections.'

'Oh yes. But leave it at that.' He waved a hand, and began to refill his pipe. 'It's not important.'

'Why did he send a possible enemy agent, and a charlatan like Lysenko? Why not one of his atomic scientists, like Sakharov?'

'Sakharov and his colleagues were otherwise engaged,' Walker said. 'As for sending me and Lysenko... I've often wondered about that myself. I suspect he sent me because he wanted the British to know. Perhaps he wanted us worried about worse threats than any that might come from him, and at the same time worried that his scientists could exploit the strange device. Lysenko – well, he was reliable, in his way, and expendable, unlike the real scientists.'

'Why did you write what you did, about Lysenko?'

'One.' Walker used his pipe as a gavel on the desk. 'I felt some gratitude to him. Two.' He tapped again. 'I appreciated the damage he was doing.'

'To Soviet science?'

'Yes, and to science generally.' He grinned. 'I was what they would call an enemy of progress. I still am. Progress is progress towards the future I saw in that thing. Let it be delayed as long as possible.'

'But you've contributed so much!'

Walker glanced around at his laden shelves. 'To palaeontology. A delightfully useless science. But you may be right. Even the struggle against progress is futile. Natural selection eliminates it. It eliminated Lysenkoism, and it will eliminate my efforts. The process is ineluctable. Don't you see, Cameron? It is not the failure of progress, the setbacks, that are to be feared. It is progress itself. The most efficient system will win in the end. The most advanced machines. And the machines, when they come into their own, will face the struggle against the other machines that are already out there in the universe. And in that struggle, anything that does not contribute to the struggle – all beauty, all knowledge, all scruple – will be discarded or eliminated. There will be nothing left but the bare will, the will to win, and the means to that end.' He sighed. 'In his own mad way, Lysenko understood that. There was a sort of quixotic nobility in his struggle against the logic of evolution, in his belief that man could humanise nature. No. Man is a brief interlude between the prehuman and the posthuman. To protract that interlude is the most we can hope for.'

He said nothing more, except to tell me that he had recommended my essay for an A++.

The gesture was kind, considering how I had provoked him, but it did me little good. I failed that year's examinations. In the summer I worked as a labourer in a nearby botanic garden, and studied hard in the evenings. In this way I made up for lost time in the areas of zoology in which I had been negligent, and re-sat the examination with success. But I maintained my interest in those theoretical areas which I'd always found most fascinating, and specialised in my final year in evolutionary genetics, to eventually graduate with First Class Honours.

I told no one of Walker's story. I did not believe it at the time, and I do not believe it now. Since the fall of the Soviet Union, many new facts have been revealed. No nuclear test ever took place at Vorkuta. There was no uranium mine at the place whose location can be deduced from Walker's account. There is no evidence that Lysenko made any unexplained trips, however brief, to the region. No rumours about a mysterious object found near a labour camp circulate even in that rumour-ridden land. As for Walker himself, his Lysenkoism was indeed about as genuine ('let us say', as Stalin might have put it) as his Marxism. There is evidence, from other and even more obscure articles of his, and from certain published and unpublished memoirs and reminiscences that I have come across over the years, that he was a Communist between 1948 and 1956. Just how this is connected with his inclusion in the New Year Honours List for 1983 ('For services to knowledge') I leave for others to speculate. The man is dead.

I owe to him, however, the interest which I developed in the relationship between, if you like, Darwinian and Lamarckian forms of inheritance. This exists, of course, not in biology but in artificial constructions. More particularly, the possibility of combining genetic algorithms with learned behaviour in neural networks suggested to me some immensely fertile possibilities. Rather to the surprise of my colleagues, I chose for my postgraduate research the then newly established field of computer science. There I found my niche, and eventually obtained a lectureship at the University of E--------, in the Department of Artificial Intelligence.

The work is slow, with many setbacks and false starts, but we're making progress.

'The Entire Immense Superstructure': An Installation

1. Daylight Passes

Verrall, you'll recall, spent only six months in Antarctica, and shortly after his return had to be talked down from the canopy of Harrods, where he seemed on the point of committing seppuku with what turned out to be a laser pointer. At the hearing he claimed to have been making an artistic statement. He opted for psychiatric treatment rather than face charges.

I visited him at the clinic, a sprawling conference-centre-style low-build on a 300-acre expanse of lawns, copses and lakes outside a small town in Bedfordshire. We walked along a gravel path, slowly – three of his toes, frostbitten after an ill-considered escapade on the Brunt Ice Shelf, were still regenerating. A minder hovered discreetly, at head level and a few paces to the side, its rotors now and then disturbing the tops of the taller plants in the beds along the path.

Verrall was silent for a while, his fists jammed in the pockets of the unfastened white towelling-robe he wore over jeans and T-shirt. From a distance he might have looked more like a clinician or technician than a patient. His beard pressed to his collar-bone, his shoulders almost touching the angles of his jaw, one foot dragging... perhaps these would have been clues to his real status.

'"Jesus lived as a human socialist",' he announced. You could hear the quotes, the portent in his voice.

'What?'

'Last night I dreamed I read that on the front cover of a celebrity gossip magazine.' He laughed. 'In the midst of all the usual stuff about who's getting married, who's been seen out with whom, who's split up, what diet she's on, et cetera.'

'What was the evidence?'

'I never read that kind of magazine in reality, let alone in dreams.'

'Have you been thinking a lot about Jesus?'

Verrall shook his head. 'Not since his death.'

'Ah.'

Suddenly he grabbed my arm – the minder lurched towards him – and pointed upward, about a quarter of the way up the sky.

'Look!'

A light moved in the blue, arcing slowly, to vanish behind a cloud.

'The Shenzhou Hotel,' Verrall said.

I could see that. 'Yes? So?'

'I don't have my contacts,' he said. He jerked his head back, indicating the clinic. 'They take them out, you know. So I'm memorising everything. Orbit times, timetables, tide tables, phases of the Moon, faces of the famous, locations of police stations, railway stations, space stations – there goes another! The Putilov Engine Works.'

It was, of course, nothing of the kind.

'Virgin Honeymoons,' I said.

'Uh-huh. Just testing.' He gave me a look like a nudge. 'At Halley we could only see the circumpolar ones. And of these, only one or two are visible in daylight. In the Antarctic night... well yeah, it's quite something. To see an orbital hotel climbing out of the aurora...' He closed his eyes and shook his head, remembering. 'You know, it was then, in the long night, that I realised. We all believed the cliché about Antarctica being the front line of the Cold Revolution. Hah!' His pointing finger tracked another daylight pass. 'The real front line is up there. LEO and geostationary, the Moon, the Earth-grazer robot mines, the foothold on Mars, the stations farther out... that's where the battle for the future is being fought. But it was the daylight passes in my last month that got to me.'

I'd heard this sort of thing before, and I'd heard enough. Verrall was not insane, his odd maunderings about Jesus notwithstanding – these I put down to an attempt to convince me, or the clinic via the minder, otherwise. Or, quite possibly, another exercise in performance art.

'That reminds me,' I said, by way of changing the subject. 'Do you wish to continue your residency?'

'I'm not in Antarctica any more.' It was like he was pointing something out.

'No,' I said, patiently. 'But the Survey gave you a grant for a year. While we expected you to stay down there for the whole twelve months, it isn't actually specified in your contract. All we need is evidence that you're engaged in producing some work inspired by your stay.'

'Well, you have that already,' he said.

'We have?'

'The Knightsbridge incident.'

I had to laugh.

'If you can justify it artistically to the committee, well...'

We continued our stroll and chat, amicably and circuitously, all the way back to the clinic's front door. I shook hands, said goodbye, and watched as he shuffled inside through the glass doors. He didn't look back. A passing waiter had an extra espresso on its tray. I let the drink cool as I sauntered down the drive to the road. As I waited to be picked up I sipped the coffee and thought over what I should report, then crushed the empty cup and chucked it in a bin that trundled past at that moment. After a minute a car pulled in and drew to a halt. The window sank into the door.

'Cambridge?' the driver asked.

'Perfect,' I said.

She jerked her thumb over her shoulder. 'Hop in.'

On the way home I filed my assessment of Verrall's mental state, and recommended that he be kept under observation.

2. Observation

Verrall wandered past Reception and into the clinic's small shop, where he bought a paper (A5, lined, spiral bound) notebook and a black gel pen. He stuffed these in the pocket of his towelling robe, and walked along two long corridors to his room. The door opened to his palm. The room was basic hotel: bed, table, chair, kettle, wardrobe, en-suite. The window gave a view across the car park and the estate to the nearby fields and woods, straddled by the local modules of the WikiThing.

Verrall boiled the kettle and made herbal tea-bag tea. He sat down at the desk and looked at the room's two cameras one by one. He shifted the chair around and placed the notebook on his crooked knee and the pen on the table. He picked up the pen and began to write, sipping the tea occasionally. What he wrote was not in the cameras' field of view.

After nineteen minutes he turned to a fresh page and stood up in front of the window. There he began to sketch the visible modules of the WikiThing, quickly and crudely, making no effort to get the angles of the tubes or the shading of the spheres right. The result looked like a child's drawing of the pieces in a giant's game of jacks, the modules carelessly connected like enchained molecules. The image was further marred by lines drawn in the wrong places and ignored or scribbled over.

He stared at the page, made a few more marks on it, with greater care and less skill, signed it, then tore out the sketch and the written pages and slid them into a hotel envelope, on which he scrawled a line. He looked directly at the camera.

'You wanted evidence of work,' he said.

He looked around the room, then took off his towelling robe and tossed it on the bed. He opened the wardrobe and put on a thick shirt and a padded jacket, and socks and boots. As he stood up in the boots he winced slightly, then adjusted the lacing of the boot on his damaged foot. He hauled a small rucksack out of the bottom of the wardrobe and stuffed the rest of his gear in it, and slipped the pen and notebook into an inside pocket of the jacket.

The door closed behind him.

A minute and a half later he appeared at the reception desk.

'I'm checking out,' he said.

'Do you mean you are discharging yourself?' said the desk.

'Yes,' said Verrall.

'Only non-interactive property can be returned to you,' said the desk.

'I'm aware of that, thanks.'

'You are not recommended to discharge yourself.'

'I know.'

'By discharging yourself,' said the desk, 'you discharge the clinic of all responsibility.'

'Good,' said Verrall.

After some seconds a minder emerged from behind the reception area and laid a transparent ziplock bag on the desk. Verrall sorted a torch, pen, watch, laser pointer, Victorinox knife, and a wallet containing only paper currency into various pockets. He left two crumpled tissues and a half-finished tube of mint sweets in the bag.

'Please place discarded items in the recycling bin,' said the desk.

Verrall complied.

'You may return at any time,' said the desk.

'I don't intend to.'

'We hope you had a pleasant and recuperative stay, and that you would recommend the clinic to others.'

'No doubt I will have occasion to,' said Verrall.

'Please sign here,' said the desk, lighting a patch.

Verrall scribbled on the patch, shouldered his pack, and walked out. A minder drifted after him.

His torn-out notebook pages arrived on my desk the following week, in a tattered envelope addressed to 'That guy Wilson from the Antarctic Survey', that had been to Cardiff (where I had an ex-girlfriend known to one of the clinic's staff) and Bristol before arriving in Cambridge. There are times when I miss postal service.

3. The Wikipedia of Things

Originating in a poorly documented, hastily conceived application of synthetic biology and genetic engineering to post-disaster emergency shelter and supply in the Flood World, seized on and mutated by criminal gangs and militias, replicating uncontrollably like some benign invasive weed, becoming a refuge for the displaced surplus population and marginal individuals everywhere, and finally reconfigured by biohackers inspired by the situationist architecture of Constant Nieuwenhuys' projected ludic social space of New Babylon – a borderless, global and polymorphic artificial modular milieu intended as the site 'of a "freedom" that for us is not the choice between many alternatives but the optimum development of the creative faculties of every human being' – the Wikipedia of Things insinuates itself across and through all previously existing environments. In an era of universal surveillance where social control is directly experienced as a quasi-divine providential good fortune, a perpetual and relentless reinforcement of the double-edged conviction that one is lucky to alive, and where all ideological contestation is instantly recuperable, the WikiThing's sheer materiality constitutes a critique made unanswerable by its silence.

It is time to make the silent modules speak, and for the very ground to rise up.

4. Interim Appraisal

There was a lot more like that.

Mary Jones, the ex-colonel who then chaired the Arts and Public Engagement Committee of the British Antarctic Survey, read through the three pages of bad handwriting and studied for a few seconds the disgraceful draughtsmanship of the sketch.

She threw the notebook pages down on her desk.

'Bastard's off his meds.'

'Off his meds, off piste, off the reservation, and off providence,' I said.

She looked startled. 'Off providence?'

'Oh yes,' I said. 'Patients have to turn in their contacts when they're admitted to the clinic. He self-discharged, so he didn't get them back.'

She blinked rapidly. 'Good Lord. How did he expect to survive?'

'He told me he was memorising timetables.'

'Timetables!'

'You know – for trains.'

'Trains.' She shook her head. 'Fucking delusional.'

'And tide tables.'

'Whatever floats your boat, I guess.'

We laughed.

'But seriously,' I said. 'I think that was just misdirection. He also claimed to be able to identify orbital structures from eye and memory, and immediately demonstrated that he didn't. No, I think... well, that screed of his suggests he's been intending to go into the WikiThing for some time. And like I said, I don't think he's insane in the least. He's not exactly feigning insanity, either. As far as he's concerned, he's still engaged on the Antarctic art project.'

'How about as far as we're concerned?'

I shrugged. 'There's not much we can do about it. Whenever he emerges from the WikiThing he'll still be living off the grant.'

'How can he do that, without contacts?'

'He took it all out in cash. He has a wad of paper in his back pocket.'

Jones frowned. 'Good luck with that. Do we have any idea where he is?'

'A minder followed him into the WikiThing, but it got eaten within seconds.'

'Okay,' she said. She stood up and stepped over to the window, gazing out at the motorway and the fields, and pointed to the inevitable strand of WikiThing in the distance. 'For all we know he could even be in there by now, just a couple of klicks away.' She sighed. 'It's frustrating.' Then she turned around sharply. 'All right. Let's take him at his word for the moment. He's being irritating and irresponsible, but what do you expect? He's an artist.'

'Yes,' I said, relieved.

'But,' she added, rapping the air with an outstretched forefinger, 'that doesn't mean you're off the hook. We don't expect our artists to churn out rabid propaganda, but we do at least expect them to produce something visible and inspiring, however avant-garde it might be.'

Before she retired from the Army and took her post at the Survey, Jones had spent most of her twenty-year service career in the Semiotics Division, some of it on the front line. (The Coca-Cola Comet stunt, rumour has it, was her idea.)

'So this' – she picked up and dropped the pages Verrall had sent – 'doesn't meet the criteria. I want to see something more substantial, and before too long, at that.'

'I'm sure you will,' I said. 'He's a very serious artist, after all.'

'So you keep telling us,' she said.

The next communication from Verrall arrived three months later, correctly addressed – airmailed, quaintly enough, blue envelope and all, and postmarked Malabo, Isla de Bioko: the capital of Equatorial Guinea, on the island formerly known as Fernando Po.

The thirty sheets of thin paper inside were typed on both sides, single-spaced, using a mechanical typewriter. I pass over Verrall's salutations and preliminary personal discourtesies and present an extract from and then summary of his narrative, with no claim as to its veracity, other than to suggest that it gives as good an explanation of subsequent events as we have yet seen.

5. Out of the Hands of Providence

My left foot hurt like fuck [Verrall wrote] but I was damned if I was going to let it show. I strode across the car park and the putting green, ignoring shouts, through (and partly over) a hedge, and into the field. I could hear the buzz of the minder a steady two metres behind me, an unbelievably annoying sound and situation, like being tailgated by a bee. Ignoring it and not looking back, quailing inwardly, I approached the WikiThing. Soggy autumn grass squelched under my boots. The nearest sphere resting on the ground had an aperture about two metres wide, a metre off the ground. Light pulsed behind the shifting rainbow sheen, as if a soap-bubble were stretched across the entrance. I climbed in. As I passed through the elliptical portal the bubble burst – the spray stung my face and the backs of my hands for an instant – then, as a backward glance showed, the sheen re-formed behind me.

Inside, banally, the bottom of the sphere was filled with soil and covered with green grass, springy as well as spring-like. The rest of sphere was transparent from the inside, though from the outside it had been merely translucent. The adjoining cylinder, likewise transparent, sloped gently upward. Just as I turned towards it, the bubble over the doorway popped again, and the minder came in. The bubble barely had time to reconstitute itself before something leapt from the grass and grappled with the minder in mid-air. The added weight brought the tiny machine to the ground in a screeching complaint of rotors. After a few moments of thrashing the new device, a sort of mechanical spider, was using four of its appendages to dismantle the minder and another four to scuttle away. It vanished into the grass – down a burrow, I guessed.

Not hanging around to investigate, I set off up the sloping cylinder. It was a good three metres in diameter, and floored with what felt like roughened plastic ridges underfoot. As I ascended I found the air becoming warm and its scent pleasant. The next sphere, well off the ground, was a kind of greenhouse, twined with creepers that seemed to sustain some hydroponic piping, from which sprouted small fruit-bearing plants, none of which were remotely familiar, in various stages of ripeness. I had no way of determining whether they were safe to eat, and I was not hungry enough to take the risk, so I hurried on.

Thereafter my progress became easier; the angular arrangement of the spheres and tubes near the clinic was replaced by a more tolerable approximation to the horizontal. Each sphere or spheroid, and some of the linking tubes, was the locale of an entirely different facility: some were greenhouses; some were rendered almost impassable with glutinous machinery from which random articles of use and ornament were exuded; others appeared to be galleries of visual art and sculpture in which I confess I lingered, though work of any discernible talent was rare. Occasionally I was faced by alternative exits from a given node; in these cases, I struck out on a generally southward course.

My wandering had taken me perhaps a dozen kilometres and three hours – the variable light, whether natural or artificial, made the passage of time difficult to ascertain, and I deliberately avoided looking at my watch – when I first heard voices ahead. The apprehension I had felt in my final steps before venturing into the WikiThing returned, redoubled. I had no idea who I might encounter. But, with a stern reminder to myself that this was a condition of the WikiThing, and that if I was not willing to face it I might as well give up my project then and there, I pressed on.

On the threshold, I paused. The space in front of me was about the size and shape of a Nissen hut, rounded at the ends. Two long tables occupied its length. About thirty people, all adults of various ages, sat around them, drinking and talking. Their clothing was eccentric or exigent. Fumes, fragrant and otherwise, drifted in visible clouds, to be whipped away by strong draughts into overhead orifices. Along the sides of the room were shelves on which cartons and cups lay, evidently the source of the drinks being consumed.

A ripple of face-turning raced down the room, and rebounded as wave of indifference and a return to the ongoing conversations. I hesitated for a moment longer, facing as I did a crowd of people whose identity and background were not just hitherto unknown to me, but impossible for me to find at a glance. And I, no doubt, was as unknown and unknowable to them.

Nerving myself, I walked into the room to make the first truly chance encounter of my adult life.

6. A Traveller in Utopia

The following entirely predictable events are then narrrated in Verrall's characteristically prolix style:

Finding among the denizens of the room an attractive woman a little younger than himself, and their conversation with each other and others present, in which Verrall expresses delight at the discovery of such interesting people and convivial company, in a milieu where the Cold Revolution no longer polarises every aspect of life, every waking thought, and contaminates our very dreams (attached sheets, 3-4)

An unnecessarily detailed and salacious account of subsequent sexual activity (sheets 5-8)

Verrall's dismay at waking to discover that the woman has vanished like a mist in the morning, like wind on the sea, and that the adjacent venue of the evening's conviviality has been transformed overnight into what appears to be a particularly strenuous gymnasium but is actually a control unit for an experimental protein folding laboratory (sheet 9)

Verrall's growing understanding of the mechanisms of the WikiThing, including sewerage, life-support, child-rearing practices, gender relations, medical procedures, laser sintering devices, quasi-pheromonal communications networks, and automated internal and external defences (sheets 10-18)

Verrall's increasing frustration with the involution and self-absorption he finds among WikiThing inhabitants in their lives of creative play (sheet 20).

His conception of an art project to subvert their complacency (sheets 20-21)

His proclamation of and concept design for New Babel, an uninhabited and uninhabitable modular tower to be built on Pico Basilé, the highest peak of Isla di Bioko (sheets 22-25).

The 'pheromonal surge' of confidence he feels that his project has propagated through the WikiThing and that thousands of eager volunteers are already making their way to Equatorial Guinea. (sheet 26)

His meticulous planning of a journey, and his departure from the WikiThing near the barely used East Coast Main Line (sheets 27-30).

I dropped to the ground [Verrall's account concludes] and walked along the railway track. Whenever a train was due, I took good care to be off the line before it came into sight. Sometimes I clambered on to a slow-moving goods train. By this and other means I reached Tilbury.

A container ship was about to leave port, headed for my destination. Timing my movements with great precision from the process chart I had memorised, I climbed up a stack of containers at the quayside, and stepped across to the adjacent stack on board just before the ship sailed.

The tide was in, as I had known it would be.

7. New Babel

Equatorial Guinea was, of course, one of the earliest sites of WikiThing deployment, initially in the form of humanitarian aid provided by the US Navy in the course of assistance to the democratic forces. The plains and rainforests of the offshore island on which the capital stands remain littered with WikiThing modules and shell fragments, as does the country's mainland territory, and many ingenious local adaptations and variations of the WikiThing as well as of the expended ordnance have been, and are being, evolved.

The growth of a spindly spike of WikiThing, eventually reaching a height of one kilometre, atop the 3000-metre summit of the dormant volcano overlooking Malabo, attracted considerable media attention. Needless to say, the Arts and Public Engagement Committee of the British Antarctic Survey followed developments closely, and with more anxiety than our responses to journalists' questions betrayed. We were able to assure inquirers that the project, though unauthorised by us, was not objected to by the Government of Equatorial Guinea, and that curiosity about it was bringing a much needed boost to tourist revenue. Some local denizens of the WikiThing – less isolated from their compatriots than are their equivalents elsewhere, and therefore in frequent if irregular communication and technically illicit trade – had been among the earliest to rally to the project. The structure itself was being self-generated from rainforest floor detritus, surplus natural gas siphoned from offshore oil wells, and volcanic debris. (I have to admit that the significance of a tall modular structure with a tough outer skin and an interior consisting largely of silicated cellulose escaped me entirely.) No damage to the environment or biodiversity of the island was being reported. We were happy to take some credit, albeit discreetly, for Verrall's project, though my increasingly urgent replies to his letter went unanswered.

It was therefore with as much disappointment as surprise that we watched the events of this February unfold. Many thousands of camera drones, aimed by reporters, tourists, agents of Western governments and Asian multiplanetary corporations, and local Equatoguinean citizens who had been alerted by street-market rumour, were on the spot (mostly at a safe distance) to record and transmit the spectacle.

It seemed at first that the dormant volcano had begun to erupt. A roar of sound rolled down the sides of the mountain. Smoke and flames boiled from the summit, around the base of New Babel. Then, more or less rapidly, the entire immense superstructure began to rise into the sky. One by one, five successive stages fell away, to combust entirely and drift down as (mostly) harmless ash.

The modules at the very tip of the spire, as is now confirmed, reached low Earth orbit, where they remain. Whether their avoidance of collision with any other structure in what is an admittedly crowded region of near-Earth space vindicates Verrall's boast that he had memorised satellite times and orbits, I can only speculate. No communication from the new satellite has been received, other than a persistent and discordant bleep which is – no doubt intentionally – reminiscent of the first Sputnik.

In the months since then, nothing further has been heard from Verrall. Claims have been made that he, with or without some confederates, actually ascended to orbit, where he or they managed to survive for some time and possibly to this day. The theoretical possibility of a closed-loop solar-powered ecology within a WikiThing module, even one of that size, does exist.

Personally, I think it far more likely that what we witnessed was an uncrewed launch, and that Verrall has once more disappeared into the WikiThing, where he may even now be hatching yet more audacious plans or (knowing him as I do) has lost interest in the project and moved on to something else entirely. But sometimes, when the remaining component of New Babel makes a visible pass above the British Isles after sunset, I look up and wonder.

Nevertheless, in conclusion: the incident passed off without endangering surface or space shipping and without incurring additional expense to the Survey. I therefore respectfully suggest that we consider the matter closed.

The Last Word

*One day | In the last year of the Obama Presidency | On the third day
of the fourth month | Shortly after the bombardment of Damascus*

the Teacher found by the roadside a fledgling fallen from its nest.

"Bad deeds vanish like the night',' Trevithick read, pausing the
app to check its latest output, "but good deeds shine forever like
the day'.'

'That's not only bogus,' I said. 'It's a brazen and pernicious
falsehood.'

'Oh, sure,' said Trevithick. 'But that's not the point, is it? We
have to submit it to the wisdom of crowds.'

He tapped Enter. The app resumed.

The wisdom of crowds, as measured by retweets and likes, left
that meme to wither on the vine.

But if the online readership didn't like it, we had others.
Thousands of them. Or rather, our app did. Later that app
acquired other names. Back then, when we were two young
coders running a shoe-string start-up out of a loft in a converted
jam factory in one of the less fashionable parts of Kirkaldy, we
called it Deepity Dawg.

*Moved by compassion | In righteous wrath | Laughing heartily
he | she
picked it up and*

141

fed it tenderly until it grew | placed it back in it in its nest | snapped its neck and

cast it in the bushes | fed it to a passing dog | roasted it

'Basically, it's a meme generator coupled with a learning algorithm,' Trevithick explained. He refrained from explaining that the learning algorithm had been cobbled together for our final exam project. 'It has a database trawled from' – he waved a hand vaguely – 'old out-of-copyright texts, and a parser to combine tropes and phrases in ostensibly meaningful ways – sayings and stories. Most of them will be junk, of course. But it sends them all out as tweets or posts, records what response they get, and refines its model. Rinse and repeat. There's more to it than totting up retweets and likes – we have quality analysis built in, credibility metrics, etc. All the SEO and social marketing packages are off-the-shelf. Our USP is the learning algorithm. That's what we're bringing to the table, and what we can offer you a one-year exclusive on.'

The Social Marketing Director of Smiles4Miles had been listening while scrolling through the detailed pitch on her tablet. She looked up, frowning.

'What's a *deepity*?' she asked.

'It's a term coined by Daniel Dennett,' I said, 'for something that's true but trivial, or profound but false. 'Love is just a word,' for example.'

'Ah. I see.'

'So,' Trevithick went on, 'the algorithm learns from the feedback to distinguish between what we call the three Ds – deep, deepity, or Dee –'

'Pack it in,' the Social Marketing Director interrupted, with a chopping rapid motion of the hand. 'We don't use that name around here.'

Smiles4Miles was a fitness motivation company: it cluttered

side shelves of high-street sportswear shops with its books, posters, videos, podcasts, apps, and apparel. The company now eyed the wider, and insatiable, spirituality and self-help markets. No wonder its directors wouldn't hear the biggest name in the woo business being bandied about.

'Bottom line,' said the Social Marketing Director, 'is that you think you can generate useful advice and inspiring quotes by natural selection?'

'Partly artificial,' Trevithick admitted. 'It takes a lot of tuning and pruning. But basically, yes.'

I could almost see the Director's thinking. What we offered was potentially worth millions. What we asked in return was peanuts. Well, peanut and raisin energy bars, but you get the picture.

So did she. She gave us a year to come up with the goods.

Perplexed| Angered | Amused | Intrigued | Overjoyed | Tearfully the followers asked: 'Why have you done this?'
The Teacher answered:

After a close scrape when we (or rather, one of Deepity Dawg's online bot army of flying monkeys) attributed some inappropriate made-up quote to Mohammed, I hand-coded a fix to replace any accidentally included names of real sages, prophets, messiahs, philosophers, rabbis, boddhisatvas and Zen masters with 'the Teacher'.

When bogus sayings, tales and homilies made up by other people, companies and bots began to be attributed to the Teacher, we knew we were on to something. When one of our original profundities turned up as the desktop wallpaper of a rival motivational company, Smiles4Miles didn't object, and nor did we. It was all grist to the algorithm's tirelessly churning mill.

The meme generator produced, of course, variant stories and sayings. Some worked, some didn't.

The algorithm learned.

The bird that the Teacher had | replaced in its nest | hand-fed for months
　　turned out to be a raven, which when fully grown
　　would eat nothing but seeds and nuts | attacked and carried off a
　　young lamb | small child.

'Take a look at this,' said Trevithick, half a year into the project. His tone was both amused and alarmed.

I scanned the discussion thread, drawn against my will into the raging debate.

'People are arguing about which sayings are *authentic*?'

'Looks like it,' said Trevithick. He snorted. 'Quite heatedly, and quite convincingly, too. They're almost swaying *me*.'

'I know what you mean,' I said. 'I feel like jumping in and shouting, 'Look, you idiots, the Teacher would never have said something as stupid as *that*''

'Even though we both know he very well could.'

'Uh-huh. He-stroke-she. *It!* A thousand lines of code that *we wrote*.'

'Have you looked through the best-of file recently?' Trevithick asked.

I nodded. 'The sayings are definitely getting deeper.'

He gave me an odd look. 'Too deep, maybe.'

I was about to reply when the phone rang. Trevithick picked it up. His answers became monosyllabic, his face stony. He rang off with a forced, false smile.

'Smiles4Miles is retrenching,' he said. 'Pulling back to the core business. And pulling the plug on us. We'll get the end-of-month payment, then that's that.'

Numbed, I gazed out of the window across the rain-darkened Firth of Forth to the bright lights of Edinburgh's business district. Not for us, now. Not unless we found a different customer, and a different business model.

'Oh well,' I said. 'Like the Teacher says, we don't need hope to persevere.'

'That wasn't the Teacher,' said Trevithick. 'It was—'

I pointed a finger at him. 'Heretic!'

We both laughed, and hit the marketing sites.

The Teacher
slew it | praised it
saying:

We found another contract, with a social search agency. I made a copy of the code, amended it, and hooked it up to different data sources – the same learning algorithm could be adapted to brand recognition and reputation as well as to inspirational messaging. Leaving the earlier version running was less trouble than switching it off.

Six months later, a reminder popped up on my screen. I'd almost forgotten Smiles4Miles.

'Is that thing still running?' Trevithick asked. 'The old Deepity Dawg?'

'I think so.' I checked. 'So it is. Might as well see what we've got.'

I opened the best-of file, and began to read. Time passed unnoticed. I returned to the present with a jolt as Trevithick, quite unprecedentedly, shook my shoulder.

'Are you all right?' He sounded anxious.

I blinked at him. 'I'm fine,' I said. 'Why do you ask?'

'You've been staring at the screen for ten minutes, with tears running down your face.'

'What? Oh.' I sniffed, blew my nose, shook my head. 'No, there's nothing wrong. I got caught up in the text. It's incredible. Our app has written a... a revelation.'

Trevithick snorted. 'I don't believe you.'

'Read it yourself.'

He did. Sometimes he laughed, sometimes he frowned and nodded. After about an hour, his eyes too trickled tears. Eventually he pulled himself together.

'You're right,' he said. 'It's a revelation. Wiser than the *Meditations*, deeper than the *Gita*, subtler than the *Tao Te Ching*, earthier than *Proverbs*, more moving than the *Apology*... and all from the wisdom of crowds.' He glowered at the server. 'That thing, that thousand lines of code has learned to push all our buttons. What does that say about us? And it's not even an AI. It's just a learning algorithm with a library, Google Books, and Twitter.'

'You know,' I mused, 'when you think what others have done with revelations so much less impressive...'

Trevithick laughed. 'All our financial worries could be over for good!'

'And our real troubles just beginning,' I pointed out. 'As the Teacher said: 'If you meet the Teacher on the road, kill him!''

'Or her,' said Trevithick, as if by reflex.

'It,' I reminded him.

We deleted all the files.

'The bird's fall was in the course of nature. Picking it up was a choice.' | 'The consequences were bad, but was the deed not merciful?' | 'Now at last the bird goes as nature intended.'

The Last Word

The Teacher found by the roadside a fledgling fallen from its nest

Fat Man in the Bardo

A clock ticks. Somewhere, a baby cries. You're in an oddly abstract space, all planes and verticals. It reminds you of a library. You don't remember ever being in a library. You remember nothing but the sudden unprovoked shove in the small of your back, and the precipitate drop. A split-second glimpse of shining railway tracks, wooden sleepers, the ingenious mechanism of points.

Then oblivion.

Now this.

Even here, in this Platonic afterlife, you're fat. You always will be fat. It defines you, eternally. You're the Fat Man. It seems unfair. You don't even remember eating.

Perspiring, thighs chafing in your ill-fitting suit, you set off in search of the crying baby. Your quest takes you around a corner, and at once you *are* in a library. It's no improvement: the maze of shelving seems endless. You take down a book, and find page after page of random letters. The next you open is blank, except for one page with a single flyspeck of comma.

You put the book back in its place and plod on. The crying diminishes. You cock your head, turn, walk to another corner and triangulate. Off you go again, with more confidence.

Around the next corner, at eye level, you meet a pair of eyes.

The eyes are connected to a brain, which hangs unsupported in mid-air. The brain is connected to a tiny, tinny-looking audio device where its chin would be if it had a skull.

'Hello,' says the brain.

'Hello,' you say. You stick out your hand, then withdraw it and wipe your palm on your thigh. Hurriedly, you introduce yourself.

'I'm the Fat Man, from' – it dawns on you – 'the Trolley Problem.'

'Pleased to meet you,' the speaker crackles. 'I'm the Brain.'

'Yes?'

'A Boltzmann brain,' it elaborates. 'A conscious human brain formed by random molecular motion in the depths of space.'

'That seems improbable.'

'*Highly* improbable!' the Brain agrees. 'But given enough space, matter and time, inevitable – unfortunately for me.' It rotates, looking around. 'We seem to be in the Library of Babel, the useless library of all possible books.' Its rotation brings its eyes back around to you, and stops. 'I keep wishing I could *blink*.'

You shrug. 'Sorry, I can't help.'

The Brain laughs. 'Count yourself lucky you're not from the thought experiment about organ donation.'

You shudder.

'Well,' says the Brain, briskly, 'let's see if we can find baby Hitler and calm him down. All this crying is getting on my nerves.'

The Brain zooms away, and you hurry after it, your thoughts catching up at the same time. Information comes to you when you need it, yet you have no memory of any life before this. It's like you're...

But you've caught up.

'That baby is *Hitler*?'

'Yes,' says the Brain, as if over its shoulder. 'Time travellers keep trying to kill him. They always fail, of course, but it's most unsettling for the child. Frankly, I fear for his future mental stability.'

From the next aisle comes the sound of footsteps, and a woman's voice:

'Loud and clear, Bob. Loud and clear.'

You sidestep between bookcases to intercept the clicking footsteps. The woman halts. She is wearing a dark blue shift-dress and black high-heeled shoes. Over her neat hairdo sits a set of headphones with a mike in front of her mouth. She looks at you with disdain and at the Brain with distaste.

You introduce yourselves. She's Alice. She keeps talking quietly to Bob, warning him against some third-party eavesdropper, Charlie. Otherwise, she's not very communicative.

Soon the three of you find the baby crying in a carved wooden cradle in a canyon of books. You look at it helplessly, then at Alice. She shoots you a baleful glare, picks up the child, and strokes and coos and pats his back. Hitler pukes on her shoulder. Then he stops bawling, but keeps looking around. His crumpled little face glowers with wary suspicion.

Once the baby's hushed, the sound that predominates is the ticking. You listen intently, trying to detect its source. Suddenly the ticking is interrupted by a scream, followed by sobs.

'Jeez!' says Alice. 'What now?'

'It's the Ticking Bomb Scenario,' says the Brain. 'Some poor devil is being tortured to reveal its location.'

'We have to stop that!' you cry.

'Why?' asks Alice, coldly. 'Do you value some terrorist's comfort over the lives of innocents?'

'*I* was innocent,' you point out. 'Nobody asked *my* opinion before shoving me to certain death.'

You and Alice glare at each other.

'Sounds like you're a Kantian and Alice is a utilitarian,' muses the Brain. 'The dignity of the individual versus the greatest good of the greatest number.'

Stand-off.

'I know!' says the Brain, brightly. 'Let's find the Ticking Bomb and turn it off ourselves!'

'Sounds like a plan,' says Alice.

The Brain rises high above the shelves, almost out of sight. It roams, rotating, then swoops back.

'Found it!' it says. 'Thirty-two minutes to go before it explodes.'

'Will we have time?' you ask.

'If we hurry.'

Hurry, you do. Alice's heels go click-click-click. Baby Hitler bounces up and down in her reluctant embrace. You're almost out of breath. The Brain darts ahead, a gruesome will-o'-the-wisp guiding you onwards.

You arrive at a wider space amid the shelving, with a table in the middle. In the middle of the table is a box, on which is mounted some kind of apparatus. A man in a white coat is observing the box. Behind the man is another man, observing the man and the box. Behind that man stands… well, you know how it goes.

From inside the box comes the sound of a cat mewling, a protest louder and more plaintive even than that of Baby Hitler.

'Should we – ?' you ask.

'No,' says the Brain. 'It would just add another layer of decoherence to the wave function.'

'Damn right,' says Alice. 'No way am I going back for that goddamn cat.'

You all hurry on, leaving Schrödinger's Cat, Schrödinger himself, Wigner, Wigner's friend and all the others to their indefinite fate. The Brain leads you around a corner and into an aisle facing a glass wall. The light is ruddy. You spare a glance outside. To the horizon stretch waste dumps, some burning. On them crawl endless human figures, salvaging junk, grubbing subsistence from garbage.

'Is that Hell?' asks Alice, sounding horrified.

'No,' the Brain calls back. 'It's trillions of people living lives barely worth living! But it's a better situation than mere *billions* of people living lives well worth living, wouldn't you agree?'

'No,' says Alice. 'I wouldn't.'

'Nor I,' you say.

'Too bad!' says the Brain. 'The reasoning is rigorous. Your revulsion is mistaken, but understandable. It's not called the Repugnant Conclusion for nothing, you know.'

You have no breath to spare for argument. Another ten minutes' jogging brings you all in front of the Ticking Bomb. The simple timer, now counting down from twelve minutes, is attached to a large cylindrical device labelled '10 kilotons'.

'Oh!' says the Brain. 'It's an atomic bomb! Does that change our views on the morality of torture?'

'No,' say you and Alice at the same moment. Baby Hitler's eyes widen and his face brightens, but he says nothing.

Alice reaches over and turns the timer back to one hour. The ticking resumes.

'Now we have time to think,' she says.

'It's interesting to reflect,' says the Brain, 'that somewhere in this library is a book containing a complete system of self-evident moral philosophy that answers all our questions. Formed out of random letters, just as I am formed out of random molecules.'

'Along with its refutation?' says Alice.

'Point,' says the Brain.

'One of us must stay here,' you say, 'and keep turning the clock back, while the others go and find the torture chamber before too many more fingernails are extracted. And then – '

'And then what?' asks Alice. 'How does that help all the poor people outside?'

'No,' you say, 'but – '

'Have you noticed how our memories work? Doesn't it strike you as odd? Try drawing something at random.'

You try to think of something. Nothing comes to mind..

'What?' you say. 'I can't think of anything I'm not thinking about.'

'Tree,' says Alice. You've never heard the word before. You sketch a tree.

'See?' says Alice. 'That's not how human memories work. That's how *computer* memories work, as I'm sure the Brain can confirm.'

'Yes,' says the Brain. 'And?'

'We aren't human minds,' says Alice. 'We're abstractions of the subjects and victims of thought experiments. This isn't a physical space, and I doubt that it's some kind of afterlife, given that none of us had *lives*. The overwhelming probability is that we're in a simulation.'

'Ah,' you say. 'But –'

'Yes,' says Alice. 'What monsters the creators of such a simulation must be!'

You and Alice look out of the window at the hellish landscape, and at each other.

'We must put a stop to this,' you say.

Alice nods. You reach for the timer at the same moment.

'Wait!' cries the Brain.

Too late.

Zero.

What the Brain was about to tell you is that there are worse possibilities than being in a simulation. The worst possibility is that this thought experiment *is* simply a possibility, but a logical one. From inside a logical possibility, there is no way to distinguish it from actuality. And a logical possibility can't be made or unmade by omnipotence itself, let alone by a ten-kiloton atomic bomb.

What the Brain doesn't know, and couldn't possibly tell you, is that there is a greater possibility: that somewhere, somehow, all the victims of all the logical possibilities including those that exist in what we laughingly call actuality can be saved, can be liberated, can be redeemed; that their suffering can be expunged as though it had never been; and that, however impossible that great, all-encompassing thought experiment may seem, or indeed be, it is nevertheless something for which you are doomed to strive, and to seek over and over again until you find it.

A clock ticks. Somewhere, a baby cries. You're in an oddly abstract space, all planes and verticals. It reminds you of a library.

[*citation needed*]

The risers of the twenty-five or so outside steps up from the esplanade to The Lie Dispensary are painted like the spines of books. Most are dystopias or other socially conscious classics: *The Women's Room, The Grapes of Wrath, The Female Man, Trainspotting…* The paint's a hard waterproof gloss, and just as well: a spring tide can swamp the Huxley and the Orwell, and storm surges splash the Atwood and shingle the Bradbury.

There's a boxy porch at the top, through which a right-angle turn to a small hallway offers the choice of an indoor stair to the roof-top restaurant, or an entrance to the right. That takes you to the café bar, from which you can go to the bookstore (straight ahead, past the bar counter) and the library (off to the left, just by the bar counter).

We usually treat guest writers to a pre-event dinner and drinks in the roof restaurant. That evening, I and my husband Mark were entertaining – or rather, being entertained by – Fred Chang. He's older than he looks in the author photos (all writers are, being generally vain and lazy) but his wrinkles emphasise the vivacity of his expressions. Getting him for a reading and signing was for us a big deal, even though two of the chain bookstores wouldn't deign to have him. 'I'm world famous,' he once said, 'in a very small world.'

In case that small world doesn't include you… Chang writes two kinds of science fiction. The first, that makes him money, is space opera. The second, that makes him famous, is offbeat speculative short stories: quirky fables which have been compared (never by him) to the space fictions of Stanislaw Lem and the 'Cosmicomics' of Italo Calvino. My own view, for what it's worth, is that he does emulate these masters in literary form but not, perhaps, in literary quality.

While we ate chips and sipped cola, Chang nibbled dim sum, glugged Tsingtao, and held forth, amusingly as ever. All the while I kept half an eye on the camera feeds in the bottom left of my specs.

Everything was going well, place filling up, yet another customer climbing the steps…

'Uh oh,' I said.

'What?' said Mark.

The man was young, lean and fit. He wore one of those leather caps with fur and flaps. Beard, fluorescent jacket, Lycra top, jeans, flashy trainers: cycle-courier type. But he ascended like an old person, step by wary step. As my gaze flicked from camera to camera, I could see that he was checking the title on each riser.

'Ministry,' I said.

'Sure?'

I twiddled a forefinger, peering at face recognition. 'Hang on.'

The name came up tardily through buffering: Victor Hutchison. Science degree. Self-employed. Age 22. But long experience – my own and my apps' – flagged that his online footprint was thin and inconsistent. The Ministry is stretched and it skimps, especially on one-shot missions: eager volunteers, in it for the credit and a small cash payment. This probably meant Hutchison was here to show their hand, not just report back.

'Excuse me,' I said, shoving my plate of chips towards Mark. I nodded to Chang – who returned my glance with a wry seen-it-all look – and picked up my cola bottle. 'Time for me to mingle.'

Hutchison paused in the boxy porch at the top to make a note, and went through to the café bar. I drifted after him. (Long hair, long skirt, both faded – I give good drift.) A dozen tables are small and round, inviting intimacy; two are long, encouraging conversation. Nearly all were occupied. Cutlery clattered, and voices loud or quiet chattered. Smells of coffee and beer and the fruity whiff of vape wafted.

Hutchison swept the room with a glance, perhaps recognising a few faces. We had a respectable sprinkling of writers and critics through the crowd tonight. He didn't clock me coming in, and passed, as far as I could tell, unrecognised. He strolled past the counter to the bookshop. Less busy than the café, it felt almost as crowded – there isn't much room to move about, except sideways. A long table with stackable chairs around it occupies the middle of the room, and for that evening yet more chairs were huddled in rows at the far end. Near the till, two young women were piling books in two columns that towered like stereo speakers at the head of the table.

Favouring the young ladies with a vague smile, Hutchison sidled past them and began a systematic survey of the stock. The books are arranged alphabetically by author. Aarons, Aaronson... Left to right, top to bottom, Hutchison worked his way crabwise from case to case and wall to wall. I chatted to our two assistants, my back to our unwelcome visitor, and watched. We have a tiny camera at the back of each shelf, its lens unnoticeable as a pin-head, and more in the ceiling. Now and then his hand darted out, snaring a suspect title – *True History of the Kelly Gang, Swimming with Seals, Lanark, One Day in the Life of Ivan Denisovich, The Moment of Eclipse, Middlesex* – to flick through the pages and put them back.

Hutchison stood up from a study of the final bottom shelf (Zelazny, Zamyatin) and ducked into the library. After a discreet moment, I followed him. Like the café, the library has tables where people eat and drink (and, at less busy times of the day, read). Like the shop, its walls are lined with shelves. The books are old, and arranged... well, I know where to find any of them.

Hutchison stood before a shelf of blue-spined paperbacks: Pelican Classics. *The Law of Freedom*, *The Wealth of Nations*, *A Vindication of the Rights of Women*, *Man versus the State*, *The Rights of Man*, *Leviathan*, *The Fable of the Bees*... He must have recognised them all from his digital check-list. I wandered among the tables, nodding and chatting to diners. He pounced on *Reflections on the Revolution in France*, turned over the first few yellowed leaves, and replaced the book.

Perhaps he was reassured by its publication date. Where does the Ministry find these people?

By the time my random walk intersected his progress around the walls, Hutchison was gazing at old linguistics textbooks. As if inadvertently, I stood beside him in a narrow gap between shelves and chair-backs, getting in his way.

'Looking for anything in particular?' I asked.

He turned from baffled scrutiny of Chomsky's *Lectures on Government and Binding*. For a moment I could measure his exact lack of interest in an old lady peering at him through round glasses. Then something clicked, whether in his recall of his briefing or (educated guess) in a drop-down menu in the folded-down peak of his cap, and his eyes widened.

'Ah!' he said. 'You must be Mrs –'

'Matilde,' I said firmly. 'So... What are you looking for, Victor?'

A flicker of bewilderment: this was probably the first time he'd been addressed by that name.

'Oh! Nothing. I'm just here for the Fred Chang event.'

'Starts in half an hour,' I said. 'We have his books on sale next door, and you have time to catch a drink.'

'I'm puzzled,' he said. 'You… circulate books like this?'

'Of course not,' I said. 'I'm a bookseller, yes, but these books aren't for sale. They don't circulate. This room is a library. My library, as it happens.'

'Do you lend them out?'

I shrugged. 'There's no law against lending books to friends.'

He frowned. 'Well actually, there is, if it's… you know, terrorist material.'

I sucked cola through the paper straw and gave him an innocent look.

'You won't find, say, the Penguins by James Connolly, Carlos Marighella, Che Guevara or Bill "Yank" Levy on these shelves,' I said.

His eyes rolled as he hurriedly looked up names, and widened as he found them.

'Anyway,' I added, edging door-ward, 'I have to attend to set-up. See you at the event, and in the meantime – enjoy your browsing!'

He almost grabbed my elbow.

'But–but suppose someone nicked any of these books? Would they be lost forever?'

'We have state-of-the-art surveillance,' I told him, over my shoulder. 'And if someone got past it, or if any of these books were otherwise removed,' – I guessed what was on his mind – 'all of lasting interest have been online for nearly a century.' Another innocent blink. 'So I'm told.'

Standing room only: about fifty. Mark conducted Fred Chang to his place. He chose not to sit, as I delivered the needs-no-introduction introduction.

Chang opened his hands to the round of applause. 'Thank you, Matilde! Thank you, Mark! Thank you, Lie Dispensary!

Thank you all!' He patted each book-stack like the heads of well-behaved children. 'My latest novel, *Blood on a Black Comet*, and my back catalogue. I hope you buy and read them, and I'll be delighted to sign afterwards. I see some new faces, and some familiar faces. Some of you, I know, have read – and heard me read from – every one of my books already. So tonight, I'd like to read from a story of mine which I can be certain none of you has read before: my work in progress, *The Regime of Truth*.'

More applause. Hutchison, halfway down the length of the table, sat up a little, eyes alert. Chang leaned forward, one hand on the seat-back, tablet in the other, and read:

'About three hundred and seventy-three light-years from Earth,' he began, in a conversational tone, 'is a small red star within whose painfully narrow habitable zone swiftly orbits a planet known, in one of the local languages, as Thrakis. The Thrakians, as they do not call themselves, are not at all like human beings. They resemble us in many ways – upright, bipedal, binocular, bisexual and so forth – but having evolved and advanced (not quite the same thing, as you must know) on a world whose day is longer than its year, where solar tides inundate and drain all land but the mountains twice a day, where these same tidal forces fuel frequent and unpredictable volcanic eruptions, and industrial global warming is difficult to distinguish from periodic brushes with the gently pulsating photosphere of the star – the Thrakians, I say, are bound to exhibit marked differences from our species in their social psychology.

'One such difference we may find difficult to credit, or even to imagine. That is: Thrakians have an inclination to believe on insufficient evidence. From the most fleeting rumour to the most elaborate structure of speculation – no matter how absurd, no matter how brief the moment or trivial the effort of thought it would take to dismiss a belief, you will find a significant number, sometimes a majority, of Thrakians believing it. Worse, having once acquired a belief, Thrakians display two unfortunate urges: to spread the belief to as many others as they can, and to resent and resist any criticism of the belief. Bizarre as we may find it, they treat an attack on their ideas as an attack on their very inmost selves.

'These inclinations – whether genetically innate or socially acquired is still a matter of (predictably impassioned and fruitless) debate – can be understood, however baffling such an alien mentality may seem to us, as a result of the hostile and unpredictable environment in which their species stumbled into self-awareness. Superstitious behaviour, fanatically held belief, and childhood obedience to adult rules no matter how arbitrary, had survival value for the individuals and groups concerned, and for the behaviour patterns themselves.

'Nevertheless, despite their harsh environment and their heavy burden of unfounded and obsolete beliefs, the Thrakians advanced by fits and starts to a high technological civilisation. Their twice-daily isolation on mountain ranges was overcome by – and indeed stimulated – improvements in transport and communication, from the log raft and the smoke signal all the way to the jet hydrofoil and the global computer network. The fundamental tenets of the scientific method of discussion – such as that any idea may be critically examined and belief should be proportioned to the evidence – became firmly established.

'But –!'

Chang paused and raised a forefinger, his gaze sweeping the audience.

'These tenets of rationality,' he went on, 'were at first only applied in science and industry. Outside these domains – even in the minds of scientists and technologists when their day's work was done – the Thrakians' deep inclination to uncritical belief raged unchecked. Word-spinning philosophers, flea-cracking ideologues, fanatics and demagogues, preachers and prophets, lawyers and politicians – in short, crooks and shysters of all kinds – continued to ply a lucrative trade.

'For many decades and centuries (by our reckoning, of course) the dichotomy was tolerated, even celebrated, and it remained in a sense tolerable. Science and technology continued to advance. However, this very advance made the inclination to uncritical belief ever more dangerous. Global communications enabled false beliefs to spread faster and farther than their refutations. Fanatics and demagogues armed themselves with ever deadlier weapons. Eventually, uncritical belief was turned on and corrupted the scientific method in the service of sinister interests – whose chief weapon was, ironically if predictably, the baseless claim that science itself was an uncritical belief system, corrupted by sinister interests!

'Eventually, after many disasters both natural and social, a new belief arose in one of the richest and mightiest realms of Thrakis. In this realm, political leaders at every level of society were drawn (far more largely than elsewhere) from the ranks of scientists, technologists, industrial managers and engineers. For reasons deep in that realm's turbulent history, the public profession of religious belief by its political leaders was so frowned upon as to be almost unheard of. Furthermore, while public avowal of the prevailing political ideals – or ideology, if you will – was de rigueur, any hint of personal sincerity in that avowal was met among the engineers and their like in the ruling circles with derision at best, suspicion at worst. Sincere belief was anything but a commendation for advancement – quite the opposite in fact!

'As time went on and older generations passed away, the rulers of that realm – and of other realms, eager to emulate what they thought was the secret of its prosperity, and sometimes outstripping their exemplars in zeal – made formal and open declaration of what had hitherto been only implicit. They decreed that henceforth, all public discussion of policy should be based only on peer-reviewed scientific evidence. The decree was rigorously enforced. All religious teachings, all speculations on Thrakian nature (so different, of course, from human nature) and all deductions from the putative natural rights of Thrakians, and suchlike fancies, were swept from the public square with an iron broom. Their place was taken by empirical social and natural science and the consequences of their results on matters of public weal. All doctrines, ideals, principles, mantras, slogans and commandments were replaced by two simple standards of discussion, dinned into the population from dawn to dusk: 'Evidence and Consequence! Evidence and Consequence!'

'Public worship, philosophical debate, and private belief went largely unmolested. But any appeal to ideas without scientific evidence in matters of public policy, and any discussion in mass and social media of their principles and any implications they might have for policy, were firmly suppressed. This became known as 'the regime of truth', and –'

At this point Hutchinson, who had become increasingly restive, sprang to his feet.

'Stop!' he cried.

There was a murmur of consternation and a clatter of chairs.

'Why?' demanded Chang.

Hutchison was shaking a little, righteousness contending with nervousness. The lad was brave, I'll give him that. It can't be easy to stand up and face the hostility of a roomful of people whose entertainment you've interrupted.

'I'm showing you the red card, Mr Chang!'

And this he literally did, flourishing the red card of the Ministry to make sure everyone saw it. Three people, I'm sorry to say, pushed back their chairs and scurried from the room, faces averted to hide their shame from themselves if no one else.

'Why?' asked Chang again, when the commotion had ceased. 'I'm merely reading a work of avowed and obvious fiction – speculative fiction, at that!'

'But it's not fiction,' Hutchison said, voice almost cracking. 'It's clearly and obviously a satire of the Ministry's public information policy.'

Chang raised his eyebrows. "Clearly and obviously'?"

'Yes, I mean come on, everybody knows…' Hutchison looked around the table, as if for confirmation.

'Prove it,' said Chang.

The after-signing drinks and arguments continued long into the evening, until we reluctantly had to call them to a halt because the tide was coming in and had reached the outside steps.

The Shadow Ministers

Jen was Defence. No way was she going to get stuck with *caring* stuff: Environment, Education, Health... Girls always got these. Jen was having none of it.

'But do you *know* anything about defence?' Sonia was First Minister, because of course. She would be Head Girl one day. You just knew it. She'd been like that since primary – since nursery, probably. This lunchtime she sat on the edge of the teacher's table, hair swaying and legs swinging. Her candidate virtual Shadow Cabinet leaned on windowsills or sat on desks. Sitting at desks would have taken deference too far.

'No more than the current Defence Minister did for real,' said Jen. She was underselling herself, a bit. Her grandfather had a shelf of paperbacks with faded covers and yellowing pages, inherited from *his* grandfather, who had been in the Home Guard: great-great-granddad's army. The old Penguin Specials had tactical suggestions. The principles were sound, the details out of date. Where now could you get petrol, or glass bottles? Jen knew better than to ask Smart-Alec. Still, there was plenty of open source material.

'I can pick it up from background. Learn on the job, like Sajid Anwar did. That's the whole idea.'

Sonia pretended to give it thought. 'Yeah, okay,' she said. She ticked the box and moved on: 'Mal? I'm thinking Energy for you?'

He looked pleased. 'Aye, fine, thanks.'

167

'Morag: Info and Comms...'

It was a Fourth Year project. The Government worried about the young: mood swings between sulking and trashing, around the baseline of having lived through the Exchanges. Live on television, even a limited nuclear war could generation-gap adolescents, studies showed. Rising seas deepened radicalisation. Civic and Democratic Engagement education challenged school students to govern a virtual Scotland, using real-time data and economic and climate models wrapped in strategy software. The authorities burned through ten IT consultancies and tens of millions of euro before a Dundee games company offered them an above-spec product for free: SimScot.

Oak Mall connected Greenock's decrepit high street to its desolate civic square. In the years after the Exchanges it flourished, literally: hanging baskets beneath every skylight, moss shelving on every wall, planters every few metres. When the floor flooded, the mall's own carbon budget couldn't be blamed.

Two days into the SimScot project. Sonia, Jen, Mal, Jase, Dani, Morag and a couple of others walked down the hill to the mall after school and mooched along to the Copper Kettle. Cruise ships arrived weekly on the Clyde like space habitats from a more advanced culture. Today the *Star of Da Nang* was docked at Ocean Terminal, a few hundred metres away. Masked, rain-caped and rucksack-laden, Vietnamese tourists ambled in huddles, glanced at display windows in puzzled disdain and bought sweets and souvenirs at pop-up stalls. The humid walkway air was itchy with midges. The café had aircon and LED overheads and polished copper counter and tabletops.

'Temptation's to treat it as a bit of a skive,' said Sonia. She drew on her soya shake, lips pursing around a paper straw. 'Check the grading, and think again.'

Everyone nodded solemnly. 'Still feels like a waste of time,' said Jase. He had plukes and pens.

'You're Education,' Sonia pointed out. 'Make me a case for dropping the requirement.'

Jase looked as if he hadn't thought of that, and made a note.

'It's like having to come up with answers to your dad's questions,' said Mal. He put on a jeering voice: '*What would you do instead? Where's the money going to come from? Yes, but what would you put in its place?*'

Jen laughed in recognition.

'Whit *wid* ye dae?' said Morag.

'Build a nuclear power station at Port Glasgow,' said Mal. He gestured at the tourists outside. 'Make a fortune recharging cruise ships.'

Sonia flicked aside a blond strand. 'Make me a case.'

'No Port Glasgow though,' said Morag. The town was adjacent to and even more post-industrial than Greenock. She was from there and kind of chippy about it. She considered options upriver. 'Maybe Langbank?'

'Speaking of nuclear,' said Jen, 'I'd start by taking back Faslane, subs and all, and then annexe the North of England as far as Sellafield.'

'Well,' said Sonia in a judicious tone, 'it could be popular...'

They all laughed. The English naval enclave across the Clyde from Greenock was a sore point.

'But not feasible,' Sonia went on. 'For one thing, breaking international law breaks the rules and gets you marked down. Like I said, Jen, what I want from you is exactly what the brief asks for: an independent non-nuclear defence policy.'

'I thought we had one already,' said Javid.

Jen had been doing her homework.

'Yes,' she said, 'if being small and defenceless is a policy.'

'Who're we defending against?' Jase demanded.

'Well,' said Jen, 'that's the big question...'

'Not for you, it isn't,' said Sonia. 'Javid's the Foreign Secretary.'

They bickered and bantered for a bit. Jen complained about toy data, and any real research getting you on terror watch-lists. Morag muttered something about a workaround for that. She picked a moment Sonia wasn't looking and slid an app across the table from her phone to Jen's.

A few minutes later Jen's phone chimed.

'Home for dinner,' she said. 'See you tomorrow, guys.'

Morag winked. 'Take care.'

Jen walked briskly up a long upward-sloping street of semi-detached houses. In one of them, at the far end, her family and five other households lived more or less on top of each other. Postwar, fast-build housing had been promised. The gaps in the streets showed the state of delivery.

A male stranger's deep voice just behind her shoulder said: 'Hi, Jen, would you like to talk?'

'Fuck off, creep.'

She leapt forward and spun around, shoulder bag in both hands and ready to shove. No one was within three metres of her. She smiled off glances from others in the homeward-hurrying crowd.

'Sorry, Jen,' said a woman's voice, behind her shoulder. 'I'm still getting used to this.'

Again no one there.

'Stop doing that!'

'Doing what?'

'Talking from behind me.'

'Sorry, again.' The voice shifted, so that it seemed to come from alongside. 'It's an aural illusion. Your phone's speakers enable it.'

'Not a feature I've ever asked for. Smart-Alec: settings.'

'Smart-Alec is inactive.'

Jen took out her phone and glared at it.

'Who are you?'

'I'm the new app your friend gave you. Call me Lexie, if you like.'

'Okay, Lexie. Now shut the fuck up.'

After dinner Jen pleaded homework and retreated to her cubicle. She slid the partition shut, cutting off sound from the living-room, and sat on her bed, back to the pillow and knees drawn up. She flipped the phone to her glasses and started poking around.

'Lexie' turned out to be an optional front-end of Iskander, which wasn't in any app store. It had much the same functions as Smart-Alec – an interface to everything, basically – but despite the clear allusion in its name it had no traceable connection with Smart-Alec's remote ancestor, Alexa. Right now, it was sitting on top of all her phone's processes, just like Smart-Alec normally did. This wasn't supposed to be possible.

She had the horrible feeling of having been pranked, or hacked. Morag didn't seem the type to pull a stunt like that. Jen had taken for granted that Morag was savvy enough not to share malware.

Jen took the glasses off and dropped her phone, watching it fall like a leaf to the duvet. She did this a few times, thinking.

'Lexie,' she said at last, 'can Smart-Alec hear us?'

'No,' said Lexie.

'What are you?'

'A user interface.'

Jen muttered about *bloody stupid literal* – 'An interface to what?

171

What is Iskander?'

'Iskander is an Anticipatory Algorithmic Artificial Intelligence, colloquially called a Triple-AI.'

'How's that different from Smart-Alec?'

'This app has different security protocols. Also, Smart-Alec can give you what you ask, and suggest what else you might want. Iskander can *anticipate* what you will want.'

Jen put her glasses back on, and poked some more. The app's source was listed, in tiny font on a deep page, as the European Committee. That sounded official.

'Okay,' she said, somewhat reassured, 'show me what you can do. Anticipate me.'

A map of Scotland unfolded in front of her. Ordnance Survey standard: satellite and aerial views, some of them real-time, overlaid with contour lines, names, symbols, labels...

Then as her gaze moved, the map highlighted all the military bases and hardware deployed in and around Scotland. Whenever her glance settled on a site, the display drilled down to details: personnel, weapons, fortifications, security procedures and on and on. She closed her eyes and swatted it away.

'I shouldn't be seeing this!'

'You wanted information on which to base an independent non-nuclear defence policy,' said Lexie, frostily. 'As you'll have gathered already, no such policy exists. Scotland is a staging area and forward base for the Alliance. The Scottish defence forces – land, sea, and air – are nothing but its auxiliaries and security guards.'

Jen had always suspected as much, and had heard or read it often enough. What she'd just seen gave chapter and verse, parts list and diagrams.

'You don't have to refer to this specifically to produce a much more comprehensive and realistic policy than you could from public information,' Lexie went on.

'Fuck off,' said Jen.

She tried to delete the app, but couldn't. This too wasn't supposed to be possible. Smart-Alec came back to the top. The classified information vanished. Iskander still lurked, to all appearances inactive – it didn't even show in Settings – but ineradicably there, a bright evil spark like an alpha emitter in a lung.

Between classes the following morning, Jen passed Morag in the corridor. 'Fight corner,' she said. 'Half twelve.'

Morag didn't look surprised.

Between the science block and the recycle bins, a few square metres were by accident or design outside camera coverage. It was where you went for fights and other rule-breaking activities. At 12:30 Jen found a couple of Juniors snogging and a Sixth Year pointedly ignoring them while taking a puff. All three fled her glower. Morag strolled up a minute later. They faced off. Morag was stocky. She walked, and carried her shoulders and elbows, like a boy looking for trouble. As far as Jen knew, this manner had so far kept Morag out of any. She had weight and strength; Jen had height and reach. She'd done martial arts in PE. Morag played rugby.

Mutual assured deterrence it was, then.

'Whit's yir problem, Jen?'

'What the fuck d'you think you're playing at?' Jen demanded in a loud whisper. 'Oh, don't give me that innocent face! You know fine well what I mean.'

'You did ask. Kind ae.'

'I did no such thing. How could I? I had no idea. Where did you get it, anyway?'

'Friend ae a friend,' said Morag, glancing aside with blatant evasiveness. She grinned. 'Had it for a while, mind. It's great! It's like a cheat code to everything.'

'Yeah, I'll bet. Meanwhile you've turned me into a spy and a hacker.'

'No if you don't tell anyone. I sure won't.'

'Christ! What about inspections?'

Morag laughed. 'It knows when to hide.'

Jen scoffed. 'Does it, aye?'

'I should know,' Morag said, smugly. 'I'm Information.'

'Is that how you got it? Researching information policy?'

'No exactly. Never you mind how I got it.' She spread her hands. 'Come on, it's all over Europe. It was bound to turn up here eventually.'

'Sounds like a new virus or a new drug.'

'It's kind ae both.'

'And who's spreading it? Who started it?'

Morag shrugged. 'The Russians?'

'We should report this.'

'What good would that do? It's still out there. The cops know about it already.'

'We should report it to the school, then. It could land us in big trouble if we don't. '

'You're the Defence Minister,' Morag jeered, 'and you go crying you've been cyber-attacked by the Russians? No a good look, is it?'

'Not as bad as the Information Minister spreading it.'

'Don't you fucking dare.'

'Dare what?

'Tell on me.'

'That's not –'

'Better fucking not.' In each other's faces, now.

Someone shouted 'Girl fight!' People gathered. Jen and Morag stepped back.

'But if you pull a stunt like that again,' Jen swore as they parted, 'I'll have you.'

She considered it, even as Morag swaggered away. Jen had never been so angry at anyone. She could turn Morag in, report the matter to the Police, just fucking *shop* the bitch and serve her right.

'You don't want to do that,' Iskander murmured, uncannily in her ear. 'You don't know what else they might find on your phone.'

Jen stood stock still and stared out across the rooftops and parks to the Firth of Clyde and the hills beyond. A destroyer's scalpel prow cut the waves towards Faslane. Kilometres away in the sky a helicopter throbbed. The *Star of Da Nang* floated majestically downriver, red flag flying. Smoke from Siberia greyed the sky.

'Don't threaten me with leaving filth on my phone,' she mouthed.

'Oh, I can do worse than that,' Lexie said. 'What you've already seen is enough to get you extradited to England, or even the US.'

'You'd turn me over to the fash?'

'If you were to betray your friend – yes, in a heartbeat.'

A bell rang. Jen slipped into the flow towards class, trying not to shake.

'On the bright side,' Lexie added, 'your friend is right. You now have a cheat code to everything. Try me.'

Jen didn't consult the illicit map again. What she'd seen was enough. She set to work devising an independent, non-nuclear defence policy for a country that was already occupied. She'd joked about taking back Faslane, but the trick would be to scrupulously respect the nuclear enclave and the other bases.

They would just have to be by-passed, while everywhere else was secured.

'Wait,' said Sonia, when she looked over Jen's first draft of a briefing paper. 'Is this a plan for territorial defence, or for an uprising?'

'They're kind of the same thing,' Jen said.

'I see you've put our national defence HQ right up against the Faslane perimeter fence.'

'Yup,' said Jen. 'Deterrence on the cheap.'

'I like your thinking.' Sonia flicked the paper back to Jen's phone. 'Carry on.'

Morag's Information policy presumed that the citizen had absolute power over what was on their phones, and that the state had absolute power to break up information monopolies. Jase on Education, and Dani on Health were likewise radical and surprising. Altogether, Sonia's team got a good grade and a commendation.

Five years later they were still a clique. They met now and then to catch up.

Jen sprinted across Clyde Square, rain rattling her hood, and pushed through swing doors under the sputtering blue neon sign of the Reserve. Mackintosh tribute panels in coloured Perspex sloshed shut behind her. Above the central Nouveau Modern bar, suspended LED lattices sketched phantom chandeliers. Drops glittered as she shook her cape dry. She stuffed it in her shoulder bag, fingered out her phone and stepped to the bar. The gang were around the big corner table. She combined a scan with a wave. Two drinks requests tabbed her glance. She ordered, and took three drinks over.

Skirts and frocks that summer were floral-printed, long and floaty or short and flirty. Jen that evening had dressed for results:

black plastic Docs, silver jeans like a chrome finish from ankle to hip, iridescent navy top that quivered as she breathed. Mal couldn't keep his eyes on her. Jen smiled around and lowered the drinks: East Coast IPA for Mal, G&T for Morag, and an Arran Blonde for herself. Sonia, elegant in long and floaty, sipped green liquid from a bulb through a slender glass coil.

'It's called Bride of Frankenstein,' she explained. 'Absinthe and crème de menthe, mostly.' Jen mimed a shudder.

Sonia's fair hair was still as long, but wavy now, or perhaps no longer straightened.

'Here tae us,' said Morag, as glasses and bottles clinked. She looked around. 'Bit of a step up from the Kettled Copper, eh?'

They all laughed, like the high-school climate-demo veterans they weren't.

'Coke and five straws, please, miss,' said Mal, in a wheedling voice.

'Oh come *on*,' said Morag. 'We never did coke, even to share.'

'Aye,' said Jase, 'we snorted powdered glass and thought ourselves lucky.'

'*Powdered* glass?' Mal guffawed. 'Luxury! In my day –'

'Guys,' Jen broke in, '*don't* fucking start that again.'

Jase leaned back, making wiping motions. 'It's dead,' he agreed. He'd lost his plukes but kept his nerdhood. Two pens in his shirt pocket, even on a night out.

'It has ceased to be,' Mal added solemnly.

Jen shot him a warning glance. He looked hard at his pint. Conversation moved on. People changed positions on the long benches. Jen chatted with Mal for a bit, then Dani, then Morag, then Javid. She zoned out, and checked the virtual scene. In her glasses ghosts moved through the crowd in the Reserve, collecting cash for the Committees. The closest of Greenock's Committees squatted an empty shop in the mall. Some people flicked money from their phones into virtual plastic buckets; others turned their backs. Jen waved away the phantom youth who approached her, then returned to the real world, where Morag was setting down a bottle in front of her.

'Thanks,' she said, eyeing Morag as she sat down beside her. Morag raised her third G&T. 'Cheers.'

'Cheers. So… how's the revolution coming along?'

'The revolution?' Morag shook her head, put her glasses on and took them off. 'Oh! The Committees? Fucked if I know, hen. I got nothing to do with them.'

'Oh come on.'

'Seriously, Jen. Like a robotics apprenticeship would leave me time for any of that! I mean don't get me wrong, France is on strike and Germany is on fire, and we all know things can't go on like this, so good luck to these guys, but what they do is full on and a heavy gig.'

'They have sympathisers.'

Morag shrugged one shoulder. 'No doubt. But not me.'

'So what changed?'

'What do you mean?'

'You remember back at school, that SimScot thing?'

'Aye, vaguely. Load a shite. Set me firm for robotics, mind.'

'You slipped me a dodgy app, remember? Called itself Iskander, or Lexie.'

'Oh, aye – you were going on about wanting to research military stuff without leaving tracks, wasn't that it?' Morag laughed. 'We nearly fell out over it.'

'Well, yeah, when I found it was showing me actual military secrets.'

'It did?' Morag's eyes widened. 'All I got was business secrets!'

'There you go,' Jen said. 'Anti-capitalist malware.'

'Do you still have it?'

'I suppose so. I could never get rid of it.'

'But you don't use it?'

'Fuck, no! Anyone who does gets flagged.'

'Ah, right.' Morag sipped her G&T. 'You're in that line now, right?'

'IT security. Yes.'

'Private?'

Jen shrugged. 'What is, these days? We get government contracts. Among others.'

'O... kay,' Morag said, voice steady as a gyroscope. 'So why are you asking me about something we did when we were kids?'

'Contact tracing,' Jen said. 'We know where the app originated. "The European Committee"! Talk about hiding in plain sight! We know how far it's spread, along with... well, the attitude that it incites. But when I look back over the records it seems that you and I were, well, pretty much Patient Zero as far as Scotland's concerned. So the question of where you got it from is exercising some minds, let's say. And for old times' sake, Morag, I'd much rather you told me than that you... had to tell someone else.'

'Like that, is it?'

'I'm sorry, but yeah.'

'Aw right.' Morag put down her glass and spread her hands, palms up, on the table. 'Honest to God, Jen, I cannae remember. I was a bad girl.' Her cheek twitched. 'Under-age drinking, under-age everything. Guys off cruise ships. Guys *on* cruise ships. I even went over to –' she jerked her thumb, indicating the other side of the Clyde '– what's legally England once or twice.'

'Fuck sake, girl.'

'You could say that.'

'So *anyway*,' said Morag, audibly moving on, 'I was damn lucky a dodgy app was the worst I picked up.'

'I'm glad,' Jen said. She grinned at Morag and raised her bottle, then drank. 'I am so fucking relieved you've cleared that up for me.'

'Cleared it up, maybe,' said Morag, grudgingly, as if not appreciating how nasty a hook she was off. 'Can't say I've narrowed it down.'

'Oh, that's all right. It'll give my clients something to work on. That's all they want.'

What Morag had told her was what she would tell them. Jen didn't care if it was true or not. It got her off the hook, too.

Morag drained her glass. Jen stood up. 'Same again?'

'Thanks.'

When she got back Morag was on the other side of the table chatting to Javid, and where Morag had been Sonia was sitting. Jen set down her own drink and looked at Sonia's mad-scientist apparatus. The green liquid was almost gone.

'Can I –?' Jen ventured.

Head turned, hair tumbling. 'Oh, thanks!'

'Another of these?'

'Christ, no!' Sonia laughed. 'I wouldn't dare.' She glanced sideways. 'I see you like your Arran Blonde. I'll try one.'

Jen returned with a second bottle. She hesitated, then plunged. 'Well, here's to blonde.'

'Here's to –' Sonia looked puzzled.

Jen laughed. 'Polychromatic.'

Sonia was in Education, whatever that meant. She'd studied and now taught at the West of Scotland University. Very much a Head Girl thing, in a way, still. It was odd to see her swigging from a bottle.

'I couldn't help overhearing what you said to Morag.' Apparently they'd got the catching up out of the way. 'You were wrong.'

'About what?'

'It isn't the Iskander app that's radicalising kids.'

That sounded like quite a lot of overhearing. 'Yeah? So what is it?'

'Apart from –?' Sonia made the helpless gesture, somewhere between a shrug and a wave of the hands, that meant *all this*. Flowery flutter around her forearms.

'Uh-huh.'

'I'll tell you a secret.' Sonia shifted closer on the bench, dress whispering. 'It's the Civic and Democratic Engagement programme. The whole idea was – well, you know what it was. It backfired, but Education think that's because something isn't quite getting across. The problem is, it is getting across! They're still doing it, wondering why every year the kids come up with more and more outrageous ideas. They keep tweaking it, but nothing works.'

Jen rocked back. 'You mean it's SimScot?'

'No,' said Sonia. 'It isn't SimScot. It's just that the whole thing of pushing teenagers to think in terms of practical policies does exactly that. Like the defence policy you came up with. Or Morag's information policy: the way the problem is posed, any answer has to be revolutionary. This keeps happening.' She let her eyelids drop. 'I see what you're thinking, Jen. Tomorrow you'll be telling someone to dig into that games company in Dundee.' Sonia's laugh pealed. 'As if!'

It is SimScot, Jen thought. She was certain of it. In the morning she would –

'I've done the research,' Sonia said. 'Real research, I mean. Peer-reviewed and published. It's the programme, not the programme, ha-ha!'

'Have you told Education?'

'Of course I've told them. They know. They listen. They take my findings seriously. And they keep doing the same thing!' She thumped the table. 'And that! Is! The Entire! Fucking! Problem!'

People were looking.

'Sorry,' said Sonia. Her voice lowered. 'Bit squiffy.'

'Blame the Bride of Frankenstein.'

'Better have some more Arran Blonde, in that case.' Sonia swigged. 'Another?'

They had another. It didn't help.

'Take me home,' Sonia said.

Sonia lived in a high flat, looking east from Greenock. As the room brightened, Jen sat sharply up from a sleepy huddle.

'What is it?' Sonia mumbled, into the pillow.

'Something just dawned on me.'

'Oh, very good,' Sonia chuckled. 'What?'

Jen gazed down at the cascade of yellow hair.

'It's you,' she said. 'It was always you. It was you all along.'

'Aw,' Sonia said. 'That's so nice.' The skin over her shoulder blade moved. Her hand brushed Jen's hip, then slipped off.

'No,' said Jen. 'That isn't what I —'

But Sonia had already gone back to sleep.

Jen waited for Sonia's breathing to become even, then rolled out of bed and padded over to the window. The wind had shifted, pushing the overnight rain back to the Atlantic. Smoke from forest fires in Germany hazed the rising sun. The sky above Port Glasgow was the colour of a hotplate, turned to a high level.

The Excommunicates

We're past the watershed now, and on the down gradient to the west. Helen slips the van into fourth gear and eases off the accelerator. The needle's at mid-tank. There's one pump between here and the coast, but whether it still works or has fuel in it is anyone's guess. I have the map across my knees, the carbine beneath it, and the binoculars bumping on my chest.

'There's an old quarry three hundred metres past the next bend,' I say. 'Best be ready to stamp on the brake or step on the gas, depending.'

'Got it.'

The windows on both sides are cranked down half-way, and the breeze comes in, heavy with a hot Highland summer. The glass is retro-fitted, supposedly bulletproof, but...

As we swing around the curve of the hill I bring up the binoculars. Hard to keep them steady, and the swoop is disorienting enough to make me nauseous, but as we approach the junction to the rutted works road leading to the great gash in the hillside, nothing seems amiss. I lower the glasses and eyeball a sweep. Heather, moss, sheep, boulders, all the way to the skyline.

'Fast,' I say.

We hurtle past the quarry mouth at 60 km/h, then slow for a long stretch of climb. Down to our left a burn trickles along the bottom of the glen, in an almost dry bed. Grey pebbles carpet the sides, amid big bare rocks.

I look down again at the map. A row of houses speckle the

roadside, two kilometres farther on, and behind and around them an irregular patch of green chequered with chevrons: coniferous woodland.

'Settlement up ahead over the hill,' I say. 'Patch of fir.'

'Ready to stamp or step,' Helen says.

I move my hand to the carbine's stock. We've drilled the move, from both seats: driver ducks, brakes; passenger brings rifle to bear; one shot, warning or otherwise; driver straightens up, hits the gas, and cranks up the window as we speed away. After much practice we have the manoeuvre down smooth – it's as awkward as it sounds – but basically we just hope we never have to use it.

My father sat between me and my sister and looked the school secretary in the eye.

'I and my family,' he said, 'are members of the Church of the Book.'

The keyboard rattled. A pair of eyebrows and reading glasses loomed above the screen.

'I can't find any reference to it,' Ms Eaton said.

'Of course not!' Dad agreed. 'That's the point.' He leaned forward, and added in a helpful tone: 'We've been called various names: the Sect of the Text, the Paper Presbytery, the Caxton Congregation...'

More keyboard rattling. 'Nothing on any of them.'

'Our West African mission has been referred to as Boko Halal.'

This was pushing it. Even I could see this was pushing it. The eyebrows lowered, and drew together. Ms Eaton leaned sideways and looked around the screen. Her lips formed a thin line.

'*Mister* Rawlins – are you being entirely serious?'

Only policy and politeness were stopping her from saying

what I could hear in her voice: *are you taking the piss?*

'Serious and sincere,' my father said. 'And our religious convictions have a right to respect, under –'

'Thank you, Mr Rawlins; I'm well aware of the relevant legislation. All right – what are these convictions, and how do they affect your children's schooling?'

'The Word of God,' my father said, 'was given to us in writing: on stone, on leaves, on parchment, on papyrus, on paper. It was not sent by email, or found on a website. We are made in his image, and enjoined to follow his example. Our Church therefore eschews electronic communication.'

'I see.' Ms Eaton sighed. 'So you don't use computers?'

'Oh, we do use computers! We're not superstitious, you know. We just don't use the Internet. For anything. No email, no web browsing, no smartphones.'

'No ebooks?'

He shook his head. 'Paper and print only, I'm afraid.'

'So they'll need physical copies of all their textbooks?'

'Yes.'

'That's inconvenient. And expensive.'

'I know. I'm sorry about that, but...'

'You're aware that some homework assignments have to be handed in electronically?'

'Of course,' Dad said. 'Liam and Melanie here can write their assignments on their own computers, and bring the files in on USB sticks.'

'What difference does...? Oh, I see.' She leaned around the screen again and gave my father a severe look, which softened as her gaze passed to us. 'I understand what this is about.'

'Thank you.'

The keyboard rattled again. 'Well, Mr Rawlins, we're required to accommodate these requirements. But we're not obliged to cover all the additional expenses. Your contribution would have to be about... 400 pounds a year.'

To me and to Melanie, this seemed an enormous sum. Looking back, it probably did to our father. He reached into an inside jacket pocket. 'I'll write you a cheque.'

Ms Rawlins looked at the strip of paper.

'Oh!' she said. 'It's like prizes. And fund-raising.'

'Exactly,' Dad said. 'Just like on the television.'

She held the cheque up to the light, and turned it this way and that. 'They're bigger on television.'

On the way home, Melanie looked up and said, 'Daddy, what's the Word of God?'

'Books some people read at weekends,' he replied.

It was the first truthful word he'd spoken on the subject.

Over the crest of the hill, and on to a longer downward slope. Again with the binoculars. No smoke rises. The houses are intact, the windows unbroken, but no washing hangs on the lines and no dogs bark. I lower the glasses, and scan the woodland around the settlement. The scent from the trees blasts in. The sun is high and everything under and between the conifers is in deep shadow.

'Step on it,' I say. As we pass the houses I catch a glimpse of something bright in the sunlight disappear around the corner of the last building: the dress of a toddler being snatched back to hiding, I guess. Still people there, but lying low. No doubt they can hear us coming from a kilometre away.

I'm just processing that glimpse when I catch another, down in the glen to our left. There's a moment of the sheer unreality of seeing a fighter jet from above, and silent as it flashes past. In the side mirror I see it vanish over the hill as the sonic boom rocks us and the engine scream catches up.

'RAF Typhoon,' Helen says.

186

'Well spotted,' I say. My heart is thumping but with surprise, not fear. It's not jets we have to worry about. I look down at the map, and seek the tiny cross that marks our first possible destination.

'Five kilometres to the nearest church,' I say.

'Pray it's an old one,' Helen says.

'Why?'

'Stone. Not some tin tabernacle.'

My laugh dies around the next bend as we see up ahead on the right a mess on the other side of the ditch, a mess that looks like a dead sheep until we see that what the crows are pecking among is a bloodied white shirt, not wool. We can't help but slow down and look, sickening though the sight is. There's nothing we can do for him or her now. In an out-flung hand, or what's left of it, the black glint of a phone screen.

'Droned,' Helen says. 'Shit. Poor bugger.'

Her knuckles are white on the wheel.

I look up at the clear blue sky, and imagine I see dots. You can't really see them. If I were to lie on the hill for a long time, and the binoculars were more powerful – stargazer standard, maybe – I might just pick out the drone swarm. Solar-powered, tiny, at a few hundred metres up, the infernal machines are known officially as sacrificial munitions platforms: aerial mines, sky-mines, murder drones, flying robot suicide bombers, call them what you like. They lurk above us by the million, right across the continent and its islands, from the Atlantic to the Dnieper. Someday, sheer wear and tear will bring them down. But long before then, they'll have destroyed every active phone and similar device that the cyber attacks and the electromagnetic pulses didn't get – and with it the phone's user, whether reckless or simply unaware of what's happened.

*

I was Bags, short for Bag-boy. Melanie, slightly luckier, got labelled Satch, for Satchel Girl. It was our first secondary school – we'd moved around a lot, and had been in and out of primary schools and what our parents called 'home-schooling'. Melanie was old enough for secondary school, and I a year older. We'd just arrived in a new town. Dad had landed a steady job at a garden centre, and Mum likewise at the local supermarket.

At first, everything went more or less fine. The big boys looked down on me from their great height. My own peers mocked me now and then for lugging books around. Sometimes they asked me about our weird religion, with more curiosity than malice. I made up doctrines and distinctions with the same glib assurance as my father habitually did. Cultural references outside my experience – online games, streamed shows – I affected to disdain or faked acquaintance with based on gleanings from review columns in the *Guardian* and the *Daily Mirror*. Ironically in view of our plight, in our house we were assiduous consumers of mainstream newspapers and the relative handful of TV channels we could access without subscriptions. Melanie and I frequented the local public library to an extent that surprised and gratified the librarians, used as they were to the almost exclusive patronage of small children and retired people.

I and Melanie did well in class, partly because we had no online distractions at home. We had books, board games, and playing outdoors. Phones and tablets were banned in the classroom, which suited us fine. Outside was where the problem arose, soon after I went through puberty and a growth spurt and became a big boy myself, 179 centimetres of gangling awkwardness. Cliques and networks, meet-ups and conflicts carried on over text messaging and apps were invisible to me. I often felt gossiped about behind my back, or frozen out of arrangements. My only extra-curricular activity was the

Orienteering Club, in which our PE teacher led us across hill and dale, using the aggressively offline navigation tools of the Silva compass, the pencil and ruler, and the Ordnance Survey map.

'You can't rely always on Google Maps,' he would say. 'Remember that.'

I remember that all right, and of course it's all moot now, but you can't always rely on Ordnance Survey maps either. The church marked by the tiny cross is a ruin, with tall old trees growing out of it.

'Ha!' says Helen. 'So much for Highland devotion!'

I could bore her with the observation that it could well have been Highland devotion that emptied that church in the first place, centuries ago. Catholic, Episcopalian, wrong kind of Presbyterian... The old Highlanders were ruthless whenever they underwent a great change in their spiritual allegiance, turning their backs on their ancient places of worship and establishing new ones. Hence the tin tabernacles, the corrugated iron sheds with nothing to distinguish them from a byre but the black notice board outside with the times of the Sabbath services and the Wednesday prayer meeting spelled out in gilt.

I decide not to bore her with Highland ecclesiastical history. Instead I look again at the map, and spot another church ten kilometres on, this time one with a spire. It's on the top of a small hill overlooking a freshwater loch, with the nearest houses two hundred metres away.

'I think we'll have better luck with the next one.'

'Any reason for thinking that?'

'None at all,' I admit. 'Just a hunch.'

'An irrational conviction, then.' Helen laughs. 'Sounds appropriate.'

Yeah, tell me about irrational convictions.

*

'Hey Bags!'

I turned. It was Claudio, a boy a year older, with whom I had not so much a friendship as a non-aggression pact, based on our shared interest in written science fiction. 'Hi, Cloudy.'

Claudio fell in with me, in my mooch around the playground. 'Got a story for you,' he said, passing me a sheaf of paper printed off from the current issue of a science fiction magazine.

'Thanks,' I said, folding the pages lengthwise and stuffing them into the inside pocket of my school blazer. 'Looks exciting.'

'You know the real reason why you can't read it online like everyone else?'

'Sure,' I said. 'The Church doesn't approve —'

'Give over. The real reason.'

'Of course I know,' I said. 'I'm not daft. We're excommunicates. My dad can't get an email address, he can't make online payments, and he can't access anything online. And my mum can't because using her identity would let him get around that, and me and Melanie can't because we aren't old enough to have our own bank accounts. The church thing is' — I shrugged — 'just a polite legal fiction so we have some cover at school.'

'But why was your dad excommunicated in the first place?'

I shot him a warning glance. 'We don't talk about it.'

'Why not?'

'You know why, Cloudy.'

'Your dad's a denier, that's why.'

A chill went through me. 'What's he supposed to be denying?'

Claudio laughed. 'Everything! Climate science. War crimes. Genocides. All kinds of atrocities.'

'And how do you know that?'

He fished out his phone, thumbed it, and showed me the

screen. My father's name, and a youthful photograph of him, headed a brief biography that gave his date and place of birth and the date of his exclusion from the online world for spreading dangerous disinformation. The types of disinformation matched Claudio's list.

'I don't believe it,' I said. 'He's not that kind of person.'

'Oh – and how would you know?'

'Know my own dad? Of course I know him. For one thing, he doesn't talk about any of that at home.'

'Yeah, yeah,' Claudio said. 'He wouldn't, would he?'

I had no answer to that. For a moment I considered telling Claudio where he could stick his science fiction story if he was going to insult my father like that, but thought better of it. With so few friends, or at least boys willing to be friendly, I couldn't afford to fall out with him.

'I'll ask him about it,' I said.

Of course, I did nothing of the sort. On the way home from school I dropped in at the public library. The librarian on the desk was one I had often noticed and eyed covertly. I'd had crushes, obviously, as kids do, but she was my first experience of hopeless, unrequited lust. She was probably ten years older than me and had neat blond hair like some elastic golden helmet framing her face and wore a nylon overall that to my overheated gaze looked like it had nothing underneath but her. I approached her as nervously as if I'd been about to ask her out on a date.

'Um, hello.'

'Yes?'

I nodded towards the row of screens and keyboards off to one side. 'Is there any way I can get online?'

'Oh! Of course. You just sign in.'

'Uh, that's the problem. I don't have an email address or anything.'

She looked perplexed. 'You don't need one. The long number on your card is your ID, and the short number is your password.'

'And that's *it*?' My voice made one of its unpredictable and unwanted pitch shifts.

'That's it!' she said, with a smile that made my face burn.

'Uh, thank you.' I smiled back for just a little too long, and turned away to the screens. I put down my laden school-bag, hung my blazer on the back of the plastic chair, grabbed the chair as it tipped backwards, sat, and tapped the two strings of numbers in.

The online world opened like a forbidden book.

Reader, I googled him.

The low hill the church stands on is a mound of glacial till, debris from the mile-high ice that carved the glen. A band of deciduous trees, birch and beech mostly, separates it from the nearest houses. The freshwater loch the hill and the houses overlook has a crannog – a tiny artificial island like a stranded stand of trees – in the middle: thousands of years older than the church, many more thousands younger than the hillock. The mountains, hundreds of millions of years older yet, wall it to north and south, and their flanks shelter it east and west. Along the far side of the loch is the old railway line; on this side pylons, one of them toppled, and three wind turbines that still spin. On a more distant hillside is a phone mast, felled.

Helen brings us to a halt in a siding cut from more of the same glacial till, like a spoil heap of rubble and gravel left over from road-building. Ten metres beyond it is the unpaved road leading up to the church. The silence is broken only by a few bleats of sheep and caws of crows, and from farther away the lowing of a cow.

Helen gives me a grim smile. 'That cow's been milked. Means

there's somebody around to milk it.'

'But not going out if they can help it.'

She nods. 'They might not even know the danger comes from using a phone. And they can't use one here anyway, with the mast down. Christ, what a mess.'

'We might even be the bringers of good news.'

'Ha! Knock on doors and say it's safe to come out?'

'More shotguns and rifles behind those doors than I'd care to chance.'

'Uh-huh.' She looks around again. 'Shall we?'

We wind up the windows, clamber out, and slide the doors to. Helen slings on her back-pack and walks around the van, locking the doors one by one. After a final check around, we walk up to the church. I carry the carbine over my shoulder, as if casually. Helen has a big knife on her belt. We stay alert.

No one is more self-righteous than a teenage boy who thinks he has his parents on the moral back foot. Few embarrassing memories are more tedious to recount than the resulting confrontations. I'll take these as read, and move to the consequences. These did not include my father mending his ways.

The problem, as he saw it, was that our cover story was too transparent. He decided to replace his thin tissue of lies with walls of solid stone. At that time there was a thing for pop-up shops: businesses that opened for a short time in unused retail premises. Pandemic, recession and war had ensured that there were lots of unused shop-fronts on every high street, and plenty of scrabbling small businesses to seek opportunity there. My father thought bigger.

He opened a pop-up church.

It was in an unused church building on a back street. For a while it had been a carpet warehouse, but that business had failed.

Nobody was opening new pubs or nightclubs that year, or the next. For five years the building had stood empty, with grass growing from cracks in the paving around its steps. The rent was derisory, almost nominal – I think the landlord or property developer was desperate for someone, anyone, to occupy the building, prevent its further deterioration, and avoid recent legislation against keeping properties empty for too long.

One Saturday not long after my fight with him, our father took me and Melanie to a DIY store. We carried small tins of paint, brushes, sheets of sandpaper, dust-masks and coveralls around a couple of corners, and there it was.

He jangled keys. 'Our church!'

Melanie clapped her hands.

While he pottered about inside, Melanie held a stepladder which I stood on. I sanded off the old sign, and gave it a fresh coat of black gloss. While it dried, we joined our father for a tea-break in the vestry, a poky room piled with carpet off-cuts and slightly foxed Bibles and hymn-books. That done, my father and I held the step-ladder while Melanie used a small paint-brush to inscribe the white lettering.

THE CHURCH OF THE BOOK
Sundays: closed
Wednesday, 7pm: weekly meeting
Minister: Jason Rawlins, MA, PhD

'Very neat,' Dad said as we all stepped back to admire it. 'Well done, Melanie!'

'Nice touch with the qualifications,' I jeered. 'Where did you get them from?'

'Edinburgh University.' He gave me a sharp look. 'What did you expect – some degree mill?'

'Well, yes,' I admitted. 'But that just makes it worse, them being real degrees.'

'Makes what worse?'

'The waste.' I scowled at him. 'A man with a doctorate, working in a garden centre!'

'It's not Dad who's to blame,' Melanie said. 'It's society's loss.'

He knew and I knew it was his loss too, and his blame. He frowned at me and smiled at Melanie. 'According to the books in there, God set the first man to work in a garden. I could do worse.'

And you did, I thought, but I kept that to myself. Melanie knew the church was an invention, of course, but she wasn't ready for the full truth yet. Our father led us back inside and set us to work sweeping the floor and dragging stacks of chairs out of a storage cupboard. We wiped dust off them and set them in concentric semi-circles, with a single chair facing them from the focus. I thanked God or whoever that the last congregation had been advanced enough to dispense with pews.

True to the notice, the first meeting was held the following Wednesday evening. The congregation consisted of me, Melanie, our mother, and three men, two of whom seemed shifty and struck me at once as creeps. The third, young and fit and with short fair hair and a frank, open face, was so obviously a cop that I almost laughed. My father took the central chair.

'The first commandment of the Church of the Book,' he said, 'is that we don't talk about why we're here. I assume that all of you' – he glanced at the frank-faced young man – 'are here because you are excommunicate, or are sympathetic to those of us who are. I don't want to hear your stories, and I'm not going to give you mine.' Good move, that. He looked around, smiling. 'This is not Excommunicates Anonymous. Sharing is not this church's mission. Its mission is something quite different. It is to preserve books. Because books will be next! You know which books I mean. I'm not talking about books illegal to possess – that's a different matter. I'm talking about books which are not banned, but whose online versions are quietly taken down. Their physical versions are unavailable in public libraries without drawing unwanted attention on the borrower or reader. Their surviving copies in private hands are fewer and fewer. You may have some of them – gathering dust! Let's share not our stories – but our books! I'm sure I would despise the books some of you most treasure. Some of you might want to burn books that mean a lot to me. In other circumstances, perhaps you would. But not in this place! Not here! Any book brought here and entrusted to me will be kept safely, and consulted freely by any adult. This church will be a library. Its second and last commandment is that we do not burn books.' He was on his feet now. 'Anyone who disagrees has no place in this church, though of course they remain welcome to listen. We may discuss these books, if we consider them worth discussing. That is all. That is the mission of the Church of the Book.'

The predictable discussion followed. Terrorist training manuals? Fascist propaganda? Pornography? 'As long as it's not illegal' was my father's answer to everything. In the weeks that followed, I was surprised and appalled to find how much that covered. This filth, that trash, these lies were *legal*?

The congregation grew. The word spread slowly: by letters, by leaflets, by word of mouth. But spread it did.

There's a low wall around the churchyard. The gate stands open, rusted in place. The grass is cropped short by sheep. Headstones are covered with moss and lichen – there have been no new burials here for decades, if not longer. But the sign beside the door is only weathered by a few years of droughts, downpours, and storms; it's still legible. Black paint and white letters:

THE CHURCH OF THE BOOK
Sundays: closed
Wednesday, 7pm: weekly meeting
Minister: Dr Alexander Singh

'Found it!' I say.

Helen grins at me. 'You had faith.'

The door is locked. Helen puts down her pack, takes out her tools, and makes short work of that. We step inside.

I met Helen online, when we were both nineteen. We'd probably never have met – she went to one of the city's other universities – if we hadn't both been online and in the same closed group: ExEx. It was for the children of excommunicates. Discussions were heated but guarded: everyone there was still careful of what they said online, and how far it might go. Despite that, she and I found we had a lot in common. Her parents had been members of the third or fourth congregation of the Church of the Book. It didn't take us long to meet in real life.

'Your father's basic fault,' she said, on our second date in the café, 'is frivolity. He isn't a fanatic for truth, or even for free speech. He doesn't believe the lies the other side puts out.'

'And your parents do?'

Helen scoffed. 'How could they, when the lies change all the time? No, they're true believers at a deeper level than that. They're onside for the other side, for God knows what reason. They think throwing out disinformation is like putting up flak – it doesn't matter how many shots miss, as long as it keeps the bombers from getting through.' She shook her head. 'Something like that. Jason Rawlins, though, he's just too mentally lazy to sort things out for himself.'

I felt stung to remonstrance. 'When we still bothered to argue... he would hit me with straight John Stuart Mill: that people who don't know the other side of an argument don't really know their own – no matter how foolish or misguided that other side may be. And that shutting people off from the other side's propaganda in the war means that deep down, many people end up not even really believing our side's news. Same with climate change, and –'

'No!' Helen leaned across the table. 'That's where you're still wrong, Liam. You still think it's an *argument*. An argument implies good faith, however mistaken one side or the other might. And there's just no good faith in what the other side puts out. There's no equivalence between the bias, the distortion, even the deceptions in our mainstream media' – she smiled at her own cliché – 'and the sort of reckless rubbish gets pumped out by state media, demagogues and populists and fossil fuel companies. That stuff is a weapon of war, and it has to be met by fighting it, not arguing with it.'

She won that argument, and she won me. In time, she won other arguments, in the profession we both chose. She formed a specialist group. When the next stage of the war came, we were ready. We had old vans with no fancy electronics, maps and compass, carbines, and all the tools to finish the job.

Inside, the church is a library. The pews are still there, but all the walls are lined with book-cases. I wander along them for a minute, seeing the familiar names of the Communists and the Fascists, the holocaust deniers, the climate change sceptics, the creationists, the racists and sexists, the antiwar right and the antiwar left. Lots of books about religious conflicts in India, from all different sides – the Sikh doctor, whoever he might have been, was clearly catholic in his choices. Alphabetical order: I find Rawlins next to Stalin, which makes me laugh. Neither would enjoy the other's company, I'll say that for them both.

Helen works the other side, then moves on to where I've just browsed. The smell of the accelerant becomes overpowering. She finishes up behind the pulpit.

'Ready?'

I nod. We go out. I toss in the match, and we wait to make sure the fire has taken hold. At the foot of the track back to the road, a tall middle-aged man stands with his arms folded, watching. He eyes the carbine, he clocks our uniforms. He nods as we pass.

'All the same,' he says, 'he was a good man, the Sikh.'

A Jura for Julia

His face was everywhere now. So it seemed to Julia, anyway, whenever she came across it. Now, on the small ferry to Jura, she could see in a single glance his portrait at the foot of a framed poster from the Ministry of Truth, and his photograph on the fifth page of today's *Sun*, left open on the coffee-slopped Formica table. The two pictures had been taken 22 years apart: one in 1989, the other in 2011.

The first showed Winston Smith as the Minister of Truth in the Provisional Government after the fall of Big Brother. Gaunt and stern, yet with compassion in the crinkles around his eyes. The recent photo showed Smith the famous novelist, journalist, telescreen personality and bon vivant: jovial, well-fed, with a shock of white hair and a neatly trimmed white beard.

The Ministry of Truth, of course, had long since been shattered into a congeries of quangos under the aegis of Public Information Services, plc. But not all of its early, urgent directives had been rescinded; and this poster, its paper yellow with age under glass yellowed by decades of cigarette smoke, remained fixed to this ship's bulkhead, as it had to the notice board of every station she'd passed through on the trains up from London. Its dire warning against spreading rumours, and the vigilance it urged against Ingsoc remnants and Big Brother loyalists, still stood.

And with good reason: in the Ladies', her hands braced to the clammy partitions as the ferry yawed and pitched on the rough sea, she'd noticed low on the door a tiny graffito in red biro: 2222. You saw that string of numbers now and then, in railway cuttings, on the walls of closed factories, on boarded-up shop windows in derelict back streets. At first she'd thought it was a date, and puzzled aloud back in London about what it portended more than two centuries hence. A comet? A predicted asteroid impact? An eclipse? But she had been laughingly set right. It was a substitution code, the simplest of all: numbers to letters.

2222. BBBB. Bring Back Big Brother.

Shocking, really, but there it was. Old habits died hard – the new oldthink, as someone had called it. People forgot, or had grown up not knowing or not believing it could have been as bad as all that.

The siren sounded. The PA system crackled, then boomed out an announcement, first in Gaelic and then in English. They had arrived.

Two cars, one large white van, and four sheep and their shepherd went ashore. Julia shouldered her rucksack, picked up her suitcase and followed the half dozen other foot passengers down the ramp. Beside a handful of houses and other buildings at the foot of a low cliff a minibus waited. Four of the other passengers boarded.

'Craighouse, please,' Julia said to the driver.

'Jura Hotel?'

'Yes.'

'Five dollars.'

She waved her miniscreen over the ticket machine, nodded vaguely to the other passengers, stowed her luggage and took her seat. The bus moved off slowly down a single track road with grass growing along its centre line. It followed the coast around the southern end of the island and on for a few more kilometres up its east side to stop at a village with a small pier and a long straggle of whitewashed houses, overlooked by the likewise whitewashed blocks of the hotel and the distillery. Julia climbed out. The driver passed her case and rucksack down. She thanked him. The bus departed.

Early October, late afternoon, overcast. Drizzle fell. A small shop was on the other side of the road. Beyond it and the pier lay a scatter of small islands. Two fishing boats, bright blue and trailing raucous flocks of gulls, were coming in. Palm trees, incongruously, grew in front of the hotel. The air carried a heavy sweetish smell, and an inconstant sough like a randomly rising and falling wind through distant trees. Julia lugged her rucksack and rolled her case up to a door marked Reception. Inside it was all dark wood and bright lights. Doors opened to a bar and restaurant, and a stairway wound upwards. No one was at the reception desk. She rang a bell and a young woman came hurrying from the bar area to stand behind the desk and switch on the deskscreen.

'Good afternoon! Do you have a reservation?'

'No,' Julia said. 'I didn't think it necessary.'

'Aye, it isn't,' said the young lady. 'Off season. How many nights?'

'Two.'

The keyboard rattled. 'Fine, you can extend that if you want.' A bright smile. 'And your name?'

'Professor Julia Hobbs.'

'And you'll be having dinner in the bar?'

Julia glanced around. The restaurant was dark, the bar bright. In the off-season, the staff were probably reluctant to open the restaurant.

'The bar's fine,' she said.

She'd made the right decision. The receptionist looked

relieved. 'There's plenty of tables, and it's not too smoky at dinner time.' She handed Julia a key on a fob. 'Room 101.'

Julia winced. The young lady didn't look like she was making a bad joke.

'Thanks,' Julia said.

'Would you like a hand with your luggage?'

'No thanks. I'm tougher than I look.'

The receptionist eyed how Julia looked.

'Aye, and so is Hamish.' The receptionist put two fingertips in her mouth and whistled. A tall young man with black curly hair and muscular shoulders strode out from the bar room, hefted the luggage, and bounded up the stairs. Julia scoffed and followed.

He stood at the door, luggage still in hand. Julia nodded downward. 'That'll be all, thanks.'

Hamish placed the luggage on the floor and made to leave. Julia tipped him a dollar, which he took with a blush.

'Thank you, Professor.'

She wasn't sure if the tip was enough or too much.

'Do you play rugby?' she asked.

'Shinty.'

'What's that?'

'It's like hockey with violence.' He paused, as if searching his memory. 'With *more* violence.'

Julia laughed. 'No doubt you can tell me all about it in the bar.'

'Aye, I'll be there.'

He ran down the stairs as fast as he had come up. Julia turned away and took her luggage into the room. She unpacked, freshened up, changed from her travel clothes into a smart frock, and went downstairs to the bar. Two old men sat in one corner, puffing on pipes. Two young men sat watching football on the telescreen. The sound was off but between them they made up for it. Hamish was behind the bar counter.

'What'll you have, Professor?'

'Half a litre of whatever local beer you recommend while I look at the menu.' He poured. She looked around. 'Uh, menu?'

Hamish pointed to a blackboard at the other end of the counter.

'Fish and chips,' she decided.

'Good choice. Fresh off the boat.' He shouted the order to the back. Julia took her drink to a table that had cutlery and condiments, sipped, and thumbed through digital mail on her miniscreen. When she'd caught up, she checked the bus timetable for the island. It was short and simple. The bus ran the entire length of Jura's one main road and back, from Feolin Ferry to where the road ran out beyond Lealt, four times a day. The first bus stopped outside the hotel at 08:20; the last one, returning, at 20:15.

The receptionist brought the fish and chips. After Julia had finished she went over to order another half-litre.

'You were right about the fish and chips,' she said.

'Carried the fish up from the pier myself.'

Nobody else was at the bar and Hamish seemed inclined to chat, so she sat on a bar stool.

'What's it like here?' she asked.

'Quiet.'

'Yes!'

'What are you a professor of, Professor?'

'Call me Julia. I'm a professor of Computational Literature at University College London.'

'Computational Literature?'

'Novels written by machines.'

'Ah, like in the Party years?'

The Party years? She hadn't heard that one before.

'Yes, exactly,' she said. She settled herself more comfortably on the stool. 'I worked on them, back then.'

'Aye, I heard they had child labour.'

'Ha! Cheap flattery will get you nowhere, young man. I was born in 1958, so I was hardly a child. I worked on the mechanical side of it – the plot kaleidoscopes, the printing and packaging and so on. I had no idea about the computations behind it all. So after the fall, I got curious about that. I had lost the sinecure the Party gave me when they were still dangling me on a string, so I got a job as a car mechanic. Then I discovered that as a former unperson I was due some compensation from the new government.' Why was she speaking so freely to a stranger? Because sometimes, she realised, a stranger was the easiest person to talk to.

'You were a political prisoner?'

Her hand went involuntarily to the now almost invisible scar on her forehead. 'I don't want to talk about that.' There were limits, even with a stranger.

'Sorry.'

'It's fine. Anyway, in 1992 I got a stipend to study. I started learning computation, and reading English literature. I wanted to understand the machines I'd been working on.' She sighed. 'The Party years were shit, don't let anyone tell you different, and for most things in everyday life fuck all worked. But in some areas that were Party priorities, the system was able to produce technology incredibly far ahead of its time. Take telescreens, for instance.' She jerked her thumb over her shoulder at the ongoing football match, still receiving loud running commentary from the lads. 'A thin flat metal screen with two-way sound and vision and universal connection! All we had to do after the fall was make them smaller, and we had deskscreens and miniscreens – a mobile telephone and more. And the speakwrite: direct transcription of text from speech! That was an accomplishment. As for machinery that could write novels – well!'

'But they were rubbish novels.'

'So they were. Trashy romances, military adventures, spy stories, crime stories, even pornography.' She grimaced. 'Beastly stuff. You don't want to know. But the technology for producing these texts was very advanced indeed. Oceania under the Ingsoc regime poured billions of dollars into machine learning, for military and surveillance purposes, and they developed what they called *large language models*, which were trained – as the jargon went – on vast quantities of written and spoken words. And where do you think they got the words from? Much of the literature of the past was destroyed in the atomic war, or under lock and key in top-secret libraries. The newspaper archives changed every day, and if you used news from one day it might get you shot the next. So what could you train the models on?'

'Ah!' Hamish said. 'The telescreens.'

'Exactly. The telescreens watched everybody and everything, and produced an incredible amount of data. Far too much for human beings to process. So they used machines for that, too, seeking out thoughtcrime. The systems, the language models were trained on that, and soon could produce convincing dialogue and narrative, once fed with a few basic plots.'

Hamish frowned. 'But if everyone knew they were being spied on all the time, wouldn't they, well, watch what they said? You wouldn't get convincing dialogue out of that.'

'You're smarter than some of my students! Yes, that was a problem, but it mainly affected people in the Outer Party. They talked in an increasingly stilted and guarded manner. Eventually, all honest and open conversation ceased, beyond trivialities. Which is one of the reasons the Party fell, and good riddance. But to return to your point – there was much more natural conversation among the proles, and that was what the models mainly drew on.'

'But the proles weren't watched.'

'That's what they thought!'

'Ah. Right.'

'So the system had a huge amount of natural conversation to draw on.' She shook her head. 'You can't imagine how vast. So although the novels were rubbish, as you say, in a certain sense they were very well written. Which made them even more pernicious, of course.'

Hamish looked sombre, then brightened. 'Could it not be used to write better novels? Does that happen now?'

'No. Not legally, anyway. We have copyright and privacy laws, after all.'

Hamish glanced at the telescreen, now showing football pundits around a studio table. 'Well… the telescreens still work both ways, no?'

'Uh huh. But they don't spy on everyone all the time. The police and security services need warrants, with specific reason in each case.'

Hamish didn't look reassured. 'Aye, right.'

'Quite.' They shared a glance; it seemed they understood each other. '*Anyway*,' Julia continued briskly, 'the machine-written literature of Oceania provides a fascinating field of study, for the likes of me anyway.'

'Each to their own, I suppose.'

'Yes. The field is not to everyone's taste, I admit. Still! It is to mine.'

'And what brings you here?'

'Oh, just taking a break. Doing a tour of the Highlands and islands.'

This was not true. Julia was seeking the sources of the most influential and genuine literary work of English Socialism: *The Theory and Practice of Oligarchical Collectivism*. Rumour had known it only as *the book*. Purportedly an analysis of the power systems of the three identical and mutually hostile blocs – Oceania, Eastasia and Eurasia – by the exiled revolutionary Emmanuel Goldstein, it had circulated underground from hand to hand. According to O'Brien of the Thought Police, it been written by the Party as a lure and a trap for secret dissenters. Neither Goldstein nor his clandestine organisation of followers, the Brotherhood, had ever really existed.

But *the book* certainly had. Julia knew that. She had seen it. She remembered Winston reading it to her. No copies of the text had ever been found. Not in the most secret caches of the dissidents, and not in the archives of the Thought Police. These had of course been ransacked after the fall of the regime, and later thoroughly searched by scholars such as herself. It was widely believed in academic circles that *the book* was a myth, and that those who remembered reading it were still suffering from delusions induced under torture by the Thought Police.

Julia knew better. She knew in her bones – which still ached sometimes – what the Thought Police could and couldn't do to induce delusions that lasted longer than a torture session. She persisted in her search, quixotic though her colleagues thought it was.

Deep in the Thought Police archives, she had come across a padlocked trunk of newspapers, books, and magazines, all charred and water-damaged and evidently retrieved from some ruin after the atomic war. Among them was a copy of the Pelican paperback of *The Managerial Revolution*, by James Burnham, a name quite unknown to her. Paper-clipped to the back cover was a cutting of a review of the book by George Orwell, another writer of whom she had never heard. Julia's glance had been caught by the word 'Eurasia', and she had read the review with mounting astonishment. At times her hands had shaken; her breath had caught. The ideas, the arguments, sometimes the very words of the review echoed or presaged those she remembered from *the book*. It was like finding a fossil bone that, by turning up in the wrong stratum, overturned an entire paleontological theory.

Further investigation in the files had turned up a few more scraps of articles, and a letter signed 'Geo. Orwell', talking about progress on a book he was writing. The letter had the writer's address: Barnhill, Isle of Jura. She'd looked it up on the OS map, and there it was, where even the track ran out at the north of the island.

Julia wasn't going to tell anyone about that, and certainly not anyone on Jura.

The football was over. Now the telescreen was showing – bloody hell, Winston Smith again, in one of those tear-jerker prolefeed programmes about finding long-lost relatives. There he was, talking to an old lady in Kingston, Jamaica who had turned out to be his aunt.

Julia finished her drink. 'Well, that's me off,' she told Hamish. 'Long day.'

'Have a good night's sleep, Julia,' Hamish said.

She did, though not unbroken. The great random sighs of the distillery ventilation helped her drift off; the roaring of red deer in rut jolted her awake once or twice, then her brain relegated it to background and stopped treating it as an alert.

She woke at 07:00 to first light on a rainy morning, kitted herself in hiking boots and trousers and waterproofs, grabbed some breakfast, packed water and bananas in her rucksack and caught the 08:20 bus. After an hour's travel along shores and hillsides and through the occasional woodland, past a few inhabited villages and the ruins of more, between the sea on her right and the mountains on her left, it reached the end of the road. There was a place where just after the hamlet of Lealt, where there was a passing place on both sides of the road, and the bus turned around.

Julia got off. Someone got on. Rain was falling. The bus trundled away. Julia set off along the untarred road towards the northern end of the island. Somewhere out in the Sound of Jura an outboard engine passed. She heard its distant hum, but in the rain she could barely make out its wake, a white line on the grey sea. An hour and a half of trudging up hill and down dale brought her to a rise from whose crest she saw below her, a few hundred metres away through the drifting rain, an isolated whitewashed farmhouse: Barnhill. Beyond it and another rise the ground fell away to the sea.

She walked down the slope. The track was so overgrown that tracing it became a matter of feeling one's way step by step between tall stands of bracken and heather. Behind her she heard a rustle, then a snort. She whirled, startled, and saw a stag not three metres away, his antlers seeming big as tree branches, his eyes glaring. She lowered her head and turned away, hurrying down the track, leaping over clumps of heather. A hundred metres on she looked over her shoulder. The stag stood on the hillside, still watching.

Julia clambered over a drystone wall up whose sides the earth had risen over decades like a slow green incoming tide. She waded through long grass past a sagging clothesline to the front porch. The door was unlocked. The hinges squeaked. She stepped inside, pushed the door closed behind her, and looked around. The windows, unwashed for years, dusty on the inside and green with algae on the outside, cast a dim light from the overcast day.

She fished a flashlight from her rucksack, and shone its beam into the corners of each room she entered. A stove with pots and pans and a kettle. A cupboard with rusty tins, and dried-out packets: flour, tea. Empty wine bottles. Full ashtrays. Empty cigarette packets. Books in stacks and heaps. No one had been in this house since before the atomic war. If anyone had been in it since, the place would have been stripped. If the Thought Police had been here not a scrap of printed matter would have been left.

She climbed the creaking stairs, testing every step before putting her weight on it. At the top she pushed open a door to a room with a bed. The covers and sheets were turned down. Patches of dark mould had spread across them. On a bedside table sat a typewriter and an ashtray full of cigarette ends. After sixty-odd years their smell had faded.

The window of this room was cleaner than those on the ground floor, and the room brighter. Julia paced, looking in every cranny. Under the bedside table was a large tin box. Julia pulled it out and used the screwdriver on her camping knife to prise open the rusted lid. Inside she found a stack of paper, the top sheet of which was blank. Perhaps they all were, and it was just a stash of typewriter paper. She picked off the top sheet to check. The next page bore the title NINETEEN EIGHTY-FOUR. It was a carbon copy, faint but legible. The next page was the typescript's first page. She read:

'It was a bright cold day in April, and the clocks were striking thirteen. Winston Smith, his chin nuzzled into his breast in an effort to escape the vile wind'

Winston Smith! Winston fucking Smith!

She lifted a big double handful of pages out and flicked through them, recognising name after name, and then her own. She found a chapter with the beginning of the text of *the book* itself, just as she remembered it. On the next few pages Winston was reading *the book* to her, or at any rate to the character named Julia. At that point she could read no further. It was too much to take in. The room seemed to be spinning around.

Julia dropped the pages back on top of the stack in the tin. Her whole body was shaking. She stood up and took several deep breaths, then let out a laugh that emerged as almost a whimper. She felt like the heroine of one of the Fiction Department's trashy novels. The melodramatic cry of 'What devilry is this?' flashed through her mind, and gave rise to a healthier laugh, this time at herself. This had to be a hoax, a forgery of some kind!

She nerved herself to read more, or at least to skim. The depiction of herself shocked her. It wasn't the physical descriptions, male-gaze though they were. It was the description of her mentality, as someone so unpolitical that she mindlessly repeated slogans she had no belief in whatever, so sensual her favoured weapon against the Party was seduction of Party members, and later so fanatical she could be a child-maiming, disease-spreading terrorist.

And then the betrayal: not what she and Winston had condemned each other to, the worst thing in the world, but the disgusted description of her in the aftermath: the thick, stiff waist. She had only skimmed the book, but she felt she had read enough.

She looked at her watch, and realised she had been reading for two hours. She had to move soon, or darkness would have fallen before she reached the stop for the last bus.

As she squatted down again to replace the manuscript, she heard the house door creak open, and footsteps in the hall. In frantic haste Julia put the lid back on the tin, stuffed the box into her rucksack, pulled the cord tight and buckled the flap. She couldn't have explained why she hid the manuscript. It was a reflex.

'Hello?' a voice called from the foot of the stairs. 'Julia? Professor Hobbs?'

It was Hamish.

Julia shouldered her rucksack, now much heavier than it had been, and walked boldly out of the bedroom.

'Yes, hello?' she called. 'I'll be down in a minute.'

She glanced into the other upstairs room, saw nothing of interest, and went down the stair. Hamish stepped aside to let her pass. They stood in the passageway staring at each other.

'What are you doing here?' Julia asked.

'I could ask you the same!'

'Oh!' Julia waved a dismissive hand. 'Idle curiosity, I'm afraid. I was coming to the end of my walk and saw this empty house and thought I'd have a poke around. Some interesting pre-war stuff here. Even the cutlery – pre-atomic steel, I'll bet. You can get good money for that.'

Hamish put his head around the front room door. He too had brought a torch, she noticed, and he shone it around. 'Aye, and books too, if the mice and the mould haven't ruined them. Looks like whoever lived here was some kind of intellectual.' He withdrew and shook his head, with a sigh. 'Christ, I wonder what happened to him.'

'Probably went to the mainland and died in the atomic bombings – Glasgow, maybe. Shame. He would have been safe here.'

'Aye, I suppose. Safe from the bombs, anyway.'

'You still haven't told me why *you're* here. Did you *follow* me?'

She realised she'd sounded more accusing than she'd intended. Hamish looked slightly abashed.

'Aye, I did that,' he said. 'Sheila – that's the lassie on Reception – told me you'd taken the bus up the island, and I checked your miniscreen's location on the deskscreen map.'

'What?'

He shrugged. 'It's routine. We're required to keep track of where our guests are on the island, in case they get into difficulties. Health and Safety. When I saw you were off the bus and headed up this track, I thought that was no walk in poor visibility for someone on their own, so I took the wee boat up here to check that you were all right.'

'That's presumptuous of you!'

'Maybe it was,' Hamish said. 'Still and all, here I am. You're welcome to a ride back in the boat, if you like.'

Julia thought of the slog back, with the new weight on her back. 'Yes, thank you,' she said. 'That would be nice.'

The rain had stopped, and the sun was breaking through the clouds, which were clearing away to the east. Julia closed the door behind them. Hamish led the way further north along the path for one and a half kilometres, mostly downhill, off the moors and through woodland to a deserted hamlet with a tiny natural harbour where a small boat was pulled well up on the shingle beach. Julia heaved her pack in and helped Hamish to get the boat back in the water. A run, a wade, a quick scissoring of the legs over the gunwale. There was a seat halfway along the boat. Julia took it, facing forward, while Hamish sat behind her at the stern. He poled the boat a short distance from shore with one of the oars, then shipped it and gunned the engine.

The boat made way not far from the shore along the Sound of Jura. Hills slid by on either side. The sun was bright and Julia had to face a little to the right to keep its glare from her eyes.

'A lot of empty houses,' she said.

'Aye, it's a sad place. Cleared by the landlords and the rest massacred or deported by the English Socialists.'

She didn't like hearing the Party called by that stolen name, but up here in Scotland (formerly Airstrip One North Terminal) she could understand why.

'You're right there,' she said. 'Seems the death squads never got to Barnhill, though.'

'Never bothered, most likely. They knew it was empty. No one there left to kill.'

'I guess.' Julia looked at another row of roofless houses on the shore, and sighed. 'And there are still people fool enough to think it wasn't that bad.'

'I've known some,' Hamish said. 'None here, though.'

She told him about the '2222' scribble she'd seen on the ferry.

'Glasgow proles,' Hamish said confidently. 'There were a lot of jobs lost when the shipyards stopped building Floating Fortresses.'

'Huh!' She didn't know what to say to that.

Hamish cleared his throat. 'If you don't mind me saying, Professor –"

'Of course not, and it's Julia –'

'Julia, back there in the house, you looked like you had seen a ghost.'

'I had.' She looked over her shoulder. 'It was my own.'

'What do you mean?'

'I found a book there – a carbon-copy of a typed manuscript.' She scoffed, to cover her perplexity at what she was about to say. 'It was a novel where I was a character, about – my past life under the old regime. Me and Winston Smith.'

'That guy off the telescreen?'

'The very same. It's all told from his point of view, it might as well have been first person.'

'Bastard!' cried Hamish. He was looking at his miniscreen while keeping one hand on the tiller.

'What?'

'It says here he was Minister of Truth in the Provisional Government.'

Julia swung her legs over the seat to face Hamish.

'That wasn't a bad thing he did,' she said. 'He fought in the uprising, and he took a responsible and dangerous post when things were still very unsettled.'

Hamish put the miniscreen away. 'Yes, yes. I didn't mean about that. I mean he must have written that book.'

'What? How?'

'Like you were saying last night. He must have used the telescreen recordings of himself and of you and other people to prompt one of those fiction-writing machines you were telling me about.'

Julia pondered this.

'I suppose he could have, or somebody else could have, and planted it here for some reason. That's the how. But it's no answer to why.'

Hamish's eyes narrowed, perhaps against the lowering sun, or perhaps in thought.

'I've read about what they did to people,' he said, in a sympathetic tone. 'Did you –?'

She thought of what she had meant when she had cried, 'Do it to Winston!' and of what she had just learned he had meant when he had cried, 'Do it to Julia!' and she felt cold all over.

'Betray each other?' Her voice was harsher and more flippant than she felt. 'Yes, we did.'

'Well then.'

Julia nodded. 'Maybe.'

It was possible. It seemed a very elaborate revenge. Were even the materials she had found in the archive forged? On the other hand, what else made sense?

Her mind went back to piece of mad metaphysics with which

her tormentor, all those years ago, had taunted her. The Party's physicists, he'd told her, had proved that the number of universes was infinite. There were infinite possible futures, and infinite possible pasts. Who was to say that the past that the Party claimed had always existed was not a real past – even *the* real past? And likewise for the past, perhaps quite different, that tomorrow it would claim had always existed?

'Doublethink is a logical consequence of the double slit,' he had gloated. She hadn't understood that at the time, but she learned what it meant later. The double slit was real, the basis of quantum mechanics. Without it no atomic bomb, no atomic war, no rise of Ingsoc…

Was it possible that in some of these infinite universes, this man George Orwell had written a book in the late 1940s that precisely, word for word, described the world that came about as a result of the atomic war of the early 1950s? If so, then his book had already been written before that world came about, and therefore existed at least in manuscript in that very world.

Yes, it was possible. No, it was too crazy.

Whatever the explanation for this manuscript's existence, there was no reason why it should continue to exist. She could open her pack and heave the tin box over the side and it would sink to the bottom of the Sound of Jura, and it would be as if it had never been.

'No, no!'

'What's wrong?' Hamish asked.

Julia shook her head. 'I didn't mean to cry out. It was… a mad thought.'

'I understand,' Hamish said. But of course he didn't.

Back at the hotel, she showered and changed and warmed up, then sat down at the room's table and read the book right through. It took her three hours. She went down to the bar for her dinner. She chose fish and chips and beer again.

When she'd finished she went up to the bar and put her empty half-litre glass on the counter.

'What'll you have?' Hamish asked.

'Something stronger.'

He gestured at the rows of bottles. 'Victoria Gin?'

It was the new branding for Victory Gin. She had been assured it was much better. She had never been inclined to find out.

'God, no.' She mimed a shudder.

'The distillery does whisky again now,' Hamish said. 'Try the 16-year-old. It's amazing.'

It was, especially with a drop or two of water. No one was around, so she talked.

'Have you decided,' Hamish asked, 'what to do with that manuscript you found?'

'Oh yes. I'm going to send it to a publisher.'

'Why?'

'It's needed now,' she said, 'and it will be as long as anyone can write "2222" and mean it.'

But that wasn't the real reason, she realised, a few Juras later. Her real reason was her own revenge. She was convinced, now, that Winston had used the fiction machines to create this book in order to get back at her.

Two could play at that game.

She wasn't shown well in the book, but he wasn't shown in a good light either. Not a good light at all. A whisky-sodden tear trickled down her cheek. The long misunderstanding was over.

She hated Winston Smith.

About the Author

Ken MacLeod was born on the Isle of Lewis and now lives in Gourock on the Firth of Clyde. He has degrees in biological sciences, worked in IT, and is now a full-time writer. He is the author of twenty novels, from *The Star Fraction* (1995) to *Beyond the Light Horizon* (May 2024) and many articles and short stories. He has taught science fiction writing at Arvon, Moniack Mhor, and Clarion West, and is a Guest of Honour at the Glasgow 2024 Worldcon.

ALSO FROM NEWCON PRESS

Best of British Science Fiction 2023 – Donna Scott

The annual showcase of British SF, now in its eighth year. The very best science fiction stories by British and British-based authors published during 2023. A thrilling blend of the cutting-edge and the traditional from Alastair Reynolds, Jaine Fenn, Stephen Baxter, Adrian Tchaikovsky, Lavie Tidhar, Ana Sun, Chris Beckett, Ian Watson, Fiona Moore, Tim Major, & more.

Selkie Summer – Ken MacLeod

A rich contemporary fantasy steeped in Celtic lore, nuclear submarines and secrets. Seeking to escape Glasgow, student Siobhan Ross takes a holiday job on Skye, only to find herself unwittingly embroiled in political intrigue and the shifting landscape of international alliances. At its heart, *Selkie Summer* is a love story: passionate, unconventional, and enchanting.

Dark Shepherd – Fred Gambino

Breel is abruptly fired from her dead-end job at the Beach, dismantling junked spaceships – a job she only took to help support her ailing father. She's convinced things can't get any worse; until people start shooting at her. A thrilling space opera that will leave readers wanting more.

Back Through the Flaming Door – Liz Williams

A new Fallow Sisters story; a new Inspector Chen story set in Singapore Three; a new tale set on the Matriarchal Mars of *Winterstrike*; a new story from the world of *Bloodmind*… All this and more in Liz Williams' stunning new collection. Thirty-two stories that enchant, dazzle, and blur genre boundaries. Take a deep breath and leap in.

To the Stars and Back – edited by Ian Whates

All new short stories and novelettes written in honour of the much-missed **Eric Brown**: (May 1960 – March 2023) by his fellow writers and friends, including Alastair Reynolds, Justina Robson, Chris Beckett, Una McCormack, Ian Watson, Tony Ballantyne, Keith Brooke, Philip Palmer, James Lovegrove, Kim Lakin, and more

www.newconpress.co.uk